"So, your clients left me something in their wills?"

The lawyer, Farnsworth, looked nervous. "Yes, my clients were two of your greatest fans. They read your column "Bringing Up Baby" every week. In fact, your love and knowledge of children added so much to their lives that…"

Devon managed to smile. "I'm sorry, but I couldn't accept anything."

Farnsworth leaned toward her with a stern look. "But you must. Everything's been taken care of. And you've been left…"

"What?"

"Amanda Phillips. She's six months old."

"A baby!" Devon managed to murmur in shock. "You're giving me a baby?"

ABOUT THE AUTHOR

In July 1995, Charlotte Douglas became an American Romance "Rising Star" with the publication of her first American Romance, *It's About Time*. Since the appearance of that debut novel, Charlotte has continued to write for American Romance and is now looking forward to the publication of her first Harlequin Intrigue. The author lives in the Tampa Bay area with her high school sweetheart whom she married over three decades ago.

Books by Charlotte Douglas

HARLEQUIN AMERICAN ROMANCE
591—IT'S ABOUT TIME

BRINGING UP BABY

Charlotte Douglas

Harlequin Books

TORONTO • NEW YORK • LONDON
AMSTERDAM • PARIS • SYDNEY • HAMBURG
STOCKHOLM • ATHENS • TOKYO • MILAN
MADRID • WARSAW • BUDAPEST • AUCKLAND

To my mother, Dorothy Harrill

ISBN 0-373-16623-0

BRINGING UP BABY

Copyright © 1996 by Charlotte H. Douglas.

This edition published by arrangement with Harlequin Books S.A.

® and ™ are trademarks of the publisher. Trademarks indicated with ® are registered in the United States Patent and Trademark Office, the Canadian Trade Marks Office and in other countries.

Printed in U.S.A.

Chapter One

A baby's tiny ears are attuned to the sound of his mother's voice. When your baby cries, murmur softly in his ear. He will cease his wailing to hear you.

Amanda Donovan, *Bringing Up Baby*

The doorbell rang for the third time. Devon Clarke ignored it, raked her fingers through her short hair and pressed Enter on her computer keyboard. The modem hummed as her fifth-anniversary column whizzed across the phone lines to the syndicate.

Satisfied, she leaned back in her desk chair. No more deadline for a week. Downstairs, the doorbell chimed again with a longer, more insistent tone.

"I hear you," she muttered. "Don't get your knickers in a knot." She slipped one foot into a sandal and groped with her toes for its mate. At the fifth irritating clamor of the bell, she abandoned her search for the other shoe, kicked off the first and trotted barefoot down the stairs. "Coming!"

The Florida sun beamed through the beveled glass panes of the front doors, silhouetting a man's rigid posture. Devon dodged sawhorses in the foyer and opened the door.

"Miss Clarke?" An elderly man with a stern expression presented his business card. "I'm Fenton J. Farnsworth. May I have a few moments of your time?"

The gray-haired elegance of the man made her conscious of her faded T-shirt, paint-splattered shorts and tousled hair. She straightened her shoulders and accepted his gold-embossed card, which identified him as an attorney from Kansas City. His expensive suit and the limousine at the curb suggested his competence at jurisprudence.

"Look—" she opened the door wide enough to display the chaos of construction in the foyer "—I'm very busy, so I'll have to pass on whatever you're selling or collecting for."

Farnsworth's starchy demeanor grew more stiff. "I assure you, I am neither selling nor soliciting. I have come in my capacity as an officer of the court to present you with a bequest."

Curiosity overrode her impatience. "From whom? I don't know anyone in Kansas City."

"But people in Kansas City, indeed all over the country, know you, Miss Clarke—or should I say, *Mrs. Donovan?*"

His disclosure of her secret identity galvanized her into action. She grabbed Farnsworth by his elbow, dragged him into the house and slammed the door behind him. In the shadows of the hallway, she jammed her fists on her hips. "Donovan's supposed to be a secret. How did you find out?"

His shrug rumpled the wool of his tailor-made jacket. "There's hardly anything I can't uncover, given enough time and resources. And my clients' resources are considerable. I suggest we sit down. You're looking a bit pale."

Devon squelched the panic that had bubbled over when he addressed her by her secret name and preceded him into the living room, zigzagging around paint cans and ladders. After tugging a dust-laden drop cloth from the sofa, she offered him a seat, and Farnsworth perched stiffly on the cushion's edge.

She sank into a chair opposite him, not bothering to remove the canvas tarp that covered it, eyed the dapper man warily and tried not to think of blackmail. She'd written under the pseudonym, Amanda Donovan, for over five years, and no one but Leona Wiggins, her agent, and her former editor, Jake Blalock, knew the real identity of the baby column's creator. "What do you want?"

He tilted back his head and chuckled. "Put yourself at ease, Miss Clarke. I don't want anything. I've come to *give* you something."

"Give me what?"

"Perhaps I'd better start at the beginning." He adjusted the gold links in his French cuffs and cleared his throat. "My clients, Chad and Gloria Phillips, owned one of the largest farm equipment corporations in the Midwest. They were two of your greatest fans. They read your column, *Bringing Up Baby,* religiously every week."

She wrinkled her forehead in confusion. "You've come all the way to Florida from Kansas City because your clients are fans of my column?"

He nodded. "Partly. Chad and Gloria wanted children more than anything in the world, and you were a source of inspiration and hope to them. After several frustratingly barren years, their daughter was finally born. And they named her Amanda, after you."

A flush of pleasure crept up her face. "I'm honored."

"Gloria said your book *Easy Meals for the Busy Mother* was a lifesaver." He smiled and smoothed his silver hair with his palm. "Your love and knowledge of children added so much to their lives, they decided to include you in their wills."

Guilt permeated her pleasure. She knew nothing about babies, never had. But she couldn't admit that to him—or anyone—because her livelihood was built on the lie. If the facts were known, her whole life, including the marvelous old Victorian house her work enabled her to make payments on, would come crashing down around her ears.

Although the bequest piqued her curiosity, she salved her guilty conscience through denial. "That was very generous of your clients, but I couldn't accept anything from them."

"But you must." Farnsworth leaned toward her with a look that must have struck fear in the hearts of his courtroom opponents. "Everything's been taken care of, all the necessary papers have been filed—here are your copies—and she'll arrive in just a few hours.''

Devon accepted the official-looking document and scanned its fine, compact print, but the legalese made no sense. Good Lord, what had they left her, a puppy? Or worse, some favorite farm animal? ''Who—or what—is *she?*''

''Your namesake, Amanda Phillips. She's six months old.''

''A baby! You're giving me a *baby?*''

He nodded.

''Not on your life, buster! You can't just waltz in here and hand me a baby, as if it was a free trip to Vegas or a set of luggage.'' She slumped back in her chair, stunned. ''Give away a child? No way.''

''Believe me, my clients wouldn't do this voluntarily. Unfortunately, they were killed in a tragic accident. Their car ran into a drainage ditch during a violent thunderstorm. They both drowned.''

At a loss for words, she stared at him. The situation left her numb with surprise, and she resisted the temptation to pinch herself, to prove the man's offer was all a crazy dream fabricated by her subconscious to punish her for deceiving her reading public.

''Fortunately,'' he added, ''the baby was at home with a sitter at the time.''

''But why choose me?'' she muttered, more to herself and fate than to Farnsworth.

''Right before Amanda's birth, Chad and Gloria named you her guardian, knowing you'd give their daughter love and expert care should anything happen to them.''

The attorney's foolishness had progressed far enough. She shoved the papers back at him. "Count me out. A child should be raised by her own flesh and blood."

"But my clients insisted—"

"Doesn't she have grandparents?"

"Deceased."

"Aunts?"

His stoic expression never wavered. He shook his head.

Desperation surged within her. "Uncles?"

"Phillips has a half brother, Ernest Potts, but the man is unprincipled. Chad and Gloria were adamant that the child be kept from him at all costs." Farnsworth pressed the guardianship papers back into her hands. "These documents are filed with the court. Returning them to me does not negate them."

Devon struggled to think. Maybe in this instance, honesty was her best policy. "Mr. Farnsworth, what I'm about to tell you is privileged information, not to be divulged to anyone."

"I understand."

"You don't want to leave Amanda Phillips with me. I'm a fraud who knows nothing about babies." Her voice squeaked like Butterfly McQueen's in *Gone with the Wind*. She swallowed hard and lowered her tone. "I was an only child, orphaned at age three and raised by a maiden great-aunt. My only experience with babies comes from reading my great-grandmother's journals, passed on by Aunt Bessie when she died. They're the source for all my writing."

He shrugged. "I fail to see a problem."

"Of course there's a problem!" She sprang to her feet and winced when her bare foot struck an errant nail. Waving her arms, she hobbled around the cluttered room. "Tons of problems! I don't know one end of a baby from another. I'm a single woman, scratching out a living for myself. And this place is full of dust, dirt and debris, no place for a child."

The attorney's calm exterior remained unruffled. "You're overreacting, Miss Clarke. All parents are beginners with their first child. It's called on-the-job training. This construction won't last forever, and Amanda's trust fund will pay for anything she needs—or desires."

"What about love? I don't love this baby, I don't know this baby, I don't *want* this baby. She needs parents who love her." A solution hit her, and she turned to face him. "Put her up for adoption."

"That would be contrary to my clients' wishes."

"What about *my* wishes?" Devon glared at him. "If I'm the child's legal guardian, I'll put her up for adoption myself, for her own good."

"I wouldn't do that if I were you." His toneless voice stopped her cold.

"Why not?"

"It would be most unfortunate if your millions of fans discover their favorite columnist has given up her own child, that she was, to use your words, a fraud."

"That's blackmail!"

"No, merely insuring that my clients' wishes for their daughter are carried out as they intended. The nurse will deliver Amanda later today, and her furniture should arrive about the same time.''

''But—''

''And this—'' he reached into his breast pocket, pulled out a slip of paper, and thrust it into her hands ''—is the first monthly payment from Amanda's trust, made out to you as her guardian.''

Devon's knees buckled at the amount, and she sank onto the nearest chair. ''That's more than I make in six months.''

''Use it for the child and for her environment.'' He glanced around the room and brushed invisible dust from his sleeve. ''As long as Amanda is healthy and happy, your secret, *Mrs. Donovan,* is safe with me.''

Devon didn't hear him leave. She sat motionless, gripping the check and guardianship papers, tangible reminders his visit hadn't been a bad dream. The check, made out to her, burned in her hand. Only a saint wouldn't feel tempted by that much money. She could pay off her house with a few more checks that size, or start a pension fund, or—she shook her head, shoving temptation away.

She wouldn't touch the baby's trust fund. It wouldn't be right—even though the extra money would come in handy each month while she waited for her check to arrive from the syndicate that distributed her columns to newspapers all over the country. No, the kid didn't belong to her and neither did the money.

She removed a tarp that covered a Windsor desk, shoved the check and papers into a cubbyhole and dropped the cloth back over the desk. Out of sight, out of mind.

The whine of a power saw across the hall dragged her from her reverie. Mr. O'Reilly had let himself in and begun work, although much later than usual. She picked her way through the maze of paint cans and debris to the kitchen door. She'd put on a pot of coffee and ask the old man for advice.

Mike O'Reilly had worked for her for the past six months, remodeling the kitchen and her upstairs bedroom first, so she could move in while he completed the renovations. She'd never had a father figure in her life, and she'd grown fond of the white-haired carpenter with his wisdom, wit and twinkling blue eyes. With Aunt Bessie gone, he was the closest thing to family she had.

The familiar atmosphere of the kitchen soothed her nerves as she scooped coffee into the basket of the coffeemaker. She'd designed the room herself with its walls and counters the color of pale sunshine, gleaming oak cabinets and lemon yellow curtains sprigged with wildflowers. She arranged homemade macadamia-nut cookies on a plate and took down two large ceramic mugs from the rack over the stove.

"Mr. O'Reilly," she called up the hallway toward the sounds of hammering in the dining room. "Coffee's ready."

She filled the mugs with the steaming brew and carried them toward the table in the dining alcove.

The sight of a tall, dark stranger in the hall doorway startled her, and she halted abruptly, sloshing hot coffee over the front of her T-shirt. "Who are you?"

The stranger hooked his thumbs in a tool belt, slung low on narrow hips over jeans that fitted like contact paper. His movement rippled the muscles of his tanned arms, exposed by the rolled sleeves of a faded denim shirt. "You didn't burn yourself, did you?"

Her skin smarted where the coffee had spilled, but her fright was greater than her injury. Huge and powerful, the man towered in the doorway. She backed toward the kitchen door. "What are you doing in my house?"

He pushed shaggy nutmeg hair off his broad forehead and studied her with eyes the color of summer thunderheads. "I'm O'Reilly."

"The hell you are!" She plunked the mugs on the table and inched closer to the exit. "O'Reilly's a white-haired old man with a big grin and periwinkle blue eyes. You're—"

"I'm what?" He fixed his generous mouth into an unyielding line above a mesmerizing cleft in his chin.

"You're—different."

An understatement if she'd ever heard one. Where O'Reilly had been kindly and slight of build, the man in the doorway radiated a strength capable of crushing her with one sweep of his muscled arm. The set of his chiseled jaw, finely sculpted nose and powerful shoulders and chest exuded a magnetism that almost made her forget the man was a trespasser.

"I'm Colin O'Reilly, Mike's son." An engaging grin cocked the corner of his mouth as he surveyed the front of her T-shirt, soaked with coffee and molded to her breasts.

She squirmed under his scrutiny, grasped the doorknob behind her and twisted, but the door was locked. She struggled with the dead bolt. "You don't look anything like Mike. I'll need identification."

With a shrug of his broad shoulders, he tugged his wallet from a back pocket, extracted a card and sauntered forward. "My driver's license."

She overcame the compelling urge to move toward him and held her ground. Her heart pounded like a jackhammer, but whether from fear or fascination, she couldn't tell. "Don't come any closer. Leave it on the table and back away."

When he slid the laminated card across the table's polished surface before stepping back into the hall doorway, her thudding heart eased its clamor. But to be safe, she unlatched the lock as she reached toward the table with her other hand. When the same intense eyes stared back at her from the photo ID of Colin O'Reilly, she experienced both relief and embarrassment.

He tucked the card back into his wallet and slid it into the pocket of his jeans. "Sorry if I startled you."

She flushed, feeling foolish. "And I'm sorry if I overreacted. You caught me by surprise."

"Dad gave me the key and told me not to disturb your writing." He strode forward and held out his hand. "I'd like some of that coffee, if there's any left."

She grasped his extended hand, and the firmness of his grip set her arm tingling. "I'm Devon Clarke. Where's Mike?"

"In the hospital."

"Hospital!" Concern for Mike swept away the last of her fear. "Why?"

"He complained of chest pains last night at home. I took him in for a series of tests. We don't have the results, but I'm afraid it's his heart." Colin unfastened his tool belt and deposited it in the dusty hall before entering the dining alcove and sitting at the round oak table.

"Poor Mike." She refilled the mugs and slid into a chair across from him. In the open plan kitchen-dining-family room, Colin seemed to fill the space, consuming all the oxygen until she struggled for breath.

Get a grip, she warned herself. Good-looking as Colin was, he was only a man, for Pete's sake. And Aunt Bessie had warned her how good-looking men could turn a girl's head and make her take leave of her senses. She shifted her gaze to the azalea bushes, wilting in the September heat outside her kitchen window, and turned her thoughts to Mike.

"Is there anything I can do for your father?"

"Thanks, but not for now. In a few days, when he's feeling better, he might enjoy some company." He bit into a cookie and lifted his eyebrows in approval. "And some cookies."

His megawatt smile almost blew her off her chair and derailed her train of thought. She fumbled for conversation to fill the uncomfortable void. "Do you live in the area?"

"Moved back last week."

"Back?"

"From Tallahassee. I closed my office there. I was planning to open one here right away, but with Dad in the hospital—" he shrugged his broad shoulders "—the office will have to wait a while."

She studied his strong square hands as he rolled the coffee mug between his palms. His well-manicured nails and uncallused fingers revealed hands unmarked by manual labor. "Office? For a carpenter?"

He smiled again, sending her blood singing. "I'm an architect—but a carpenter, too. Dad put a hammer and saw in my hands as soon as I was old enough to walk. I suppose you're concerned about your house?"

Baby Amanda would be arriving in a few hours, and she had no idea what to do with her. Her body had turned on her, reacting to the man across from her like a teenager caught in a hormonal tsunami. A hiatus in her remodeling plans was the least of her worries. "No, not really—"

"You're not canceling the work?"

"It can wait until Mike's better."

A stillness descended on him, and he stared out the bay window at the back lawn. The only sounds in the room were the tick of an old-fashioned day clock and the hiss of her own breathing.

When he turned to face her, pain clouded his eyes. "Dad's working days may be over. If his ticker's bad, he'll have to take life easy."

"I'm sorry. That will be hard for him."

Colin nodded. "He's conscientious and proud. And he's worried about you—asked me to finish this job for him."

The thought of Colin O'Reilly in her house for the next several months threw her further into panic. Would she grow accustomed to him or would he continue to unsettle her, distracting her from her work? Baby Amanda would be distraction enough.

"I don't know, Mr. O'Reilly—"

"Colin."

She was drowning in the liquid steel of his eyes. Her thoughts whirled; her mind wouldn't focus. "You see, I'm expecting a baby."

His gaze flickered to her flat stomach. "Congratulations."

"But I'm getting rid of it."

His jaw hardened. "I see."

"No, it's not what you—" The doorbell chimed. "Good Lord, she's here already."

"Heaven save me from crazy women," he muttered, rolling his eyes.

She leaped up, knocked over the ladder-back chair, scurried up the hall and flung open the front door.

A matronly woman stood on the front porch with an infant car seat in her arms. "Mrs. Donovan, here's your baby, all safe and sound."

Big brown eyes stared at her from beneath the turned-up brim of a pink hat. Chubby arms and legs protruded from a pink sunsuit and flailed the air. The matron shoved the carrier into Devon's arms, and she clutched it awkwardly, terrified of dropping the wiggling bundle. Her initial admiration of the cuddly child hardened into a knot of unadulterated panic deep in her gut.

"Her diapers and formula are here." The woman plunked a large bag at Devon's feet. "The van will arrive shortly with the rest of her things."

A thousand questions surged through Devon's head. "But when do I feed her? How—"

The woman started down the steps and called over her shoulder, "My instructions were to deliver the child. The rest is up to you."

"Wait—"

But the woman continued to her car, climbed in and sped away, leaving Devon standing on the porch with Amanda wriggling in the carrier in her arms. She headed back into the house and bumped into Colin in the front hallway.

He nodded toward the child. "That was fast work."

"You have no idea," Devon said, scowling at him.

When he leaned over the child, his face softened. "She's a sweetheart."

Devon studied the plump, dimpled face. Amanda stared back at her with round eyes, screwed her tiny features into a scowl, opened her toothless mouth and screamed in a frantic, high-pitched howl.

Remembering Gramma Donovan's advice in the column she'd just finished, Devon lowered her lips to the baby's ear and crooned, "It's all right, kiddo, Devon will take care of you."

Small fists grabbed her hair and yanked, bringing tears to her eyes. The more Devon murmured, the harder Amanda pulled on her hair and the louder the baby's howls crescendoed, echoing across the empty rooms. Through the captured strands of hair pulled taut across her eyes, she spotted Colin, who had followed her down the hall.

"Don't just stand there," she cried. "Make her turn me loose."

Colin bit back a laugh at the panic on Devon's face and gently pried the tiny fingers from her hair. Devon Clarke was one surprise after another. When his father had described her as a single woman and a writer, Colin had pictured an unattractive spinster quite a bit older.

The sight of her lithe, trim body clad in shorts that revealed long, supple legs and a damp, clinging shirt that left nothing to his imagination had been a very pleasant shock. And her pixie face had almost defrosted the glacier Felicia had made of his heart.

Those pools of gold-flecked green filled with terror as she juggled the crying baby in her arms and dodged the waving fists that continued to grab for her hair.

"Here," he said, "give her to me."

Without hesitation, Devon thrust the baby at him. "Take her into the kitchen, out of this dust."

He removed the child from its carrier, and she snuggled into the crook of his arm, hiccupped and grew quiet, assessing him with smiling eyes. The tug on his heartstrings brought moisture to his eyes, and he cursed Felicia again for her change of heart, her refusal to consider having children. For years he'd longed for a child of his own to fit as naturally in his arms as this small stranger did.

Devon tucked the car seat under one arm, hefted the large bag over her shoulder and led the way back through the kitchen into the adjoining sitting area. She piled the baby's belongings on the kitchen counter.

Colin settled into a bentwood chair by the fireplace and began to rock. The baby's eyes drooped and fluttered before closing altogether.

Devon nestled into the corner of the sofa and curled her long legs beneath her. "How did you do that?"

"Do what?"

"Make her stop crying."

He couldn't decide who was more appealing—the child in his arms or the woman who stared at him with wide eyes in a heart-shaped face. "You don't have much experience with babies, do you?"

"Absolutely zip."

He shifted Amanda's weight and continued rocking. "Babies rely on nonverbal clues for communication. The tension in your body relayed your uneasiness. When babies are afraid, they cry to let you know it."

Her eyes never left the baby's face, and he could read a latent fascination through her apprehension.

"So when you took her," Devon said, "she relaxed because you did. How do you know so much about babies? Do you have children of your own?"

He repressed the pain that pierced him at her question and shook his head. "I come from a big family with four younger brothers and sisters. Seemed like there was always a baby in the house."

The rocking motion of the chair and the weight of the small, warm body eased some of the bitterness that had gripped him since his divorce. The homey atmosphere of the big kitchen, the child clutched against his heart and the beautiful woman across from him—this had been his dream, a dream Felicia had shattered with her selfishness.

"What am I going to do with her?" Devon asked.

"She'll need feeding before long." He slipped a finger beneath the elastic of her plastic pants. "And changing."

Devon jumped to her bare feet and paced before the fireplace, running long, elegant fingers through her short curls. "That's not what I meant. What am I going to *do* with her?"

"You raise her the best you can." He couldn't keep the impatience from his voice. Had all women become so liberated they'd turned their backs on motherhood? "She is yours, isn't she?"

She stopped pacing and plopped onto the sofa with her legs stretched before her, her chin resting on her chest. "Legally, yes. Morally, I don't know."

"Miss Clarke—"

"Devon."

"Devon, you're talking in riddles. Is this baby yours or not?"

"According to Fenton J. Farnsworth, attorney-at-law, her parents, now deceased, named me her guardian in their wills."

"That settles it, then." He squelched the urge to shake some sense into her very pretty head. "They must have thought highly of you to leave you their most precious possession.''

She leaned against the backrest and stared at the ceiling. ''Her parents didn't know me from Adam. We never met.''

''Then how—''

''I'm a writer. They read my weekly columns in the newspaper and liked my style.'' When she turned toward him, worry clouded her eyes. ''Now do you see my dilemma?''

He nodded, then realized the warmth spreading across his sleeve was more than the baby's body temperature. ''Are there any diapers in that bag?''

Devon unzipped the large carryall, found only cloth diapers and handed him one.

''Uh-uh.'' He stood and offered her the child. ''You have to learn sometime.''

The loud ring of the telephone saved her. ''Next time, okay?''

She thrust the diaper into his hands, rushed to the wall phone above the kitchen desk and grabbed the receiver.

''Devon, I have terrific news.'' The voice of Leona Wiggins, her agent in New York, vibrated in her ear. ''I've just had a call from the producer of 'The Sara Davis Show.' Sara wants to do an interview with you for her Christmas special, the whole hour-long show.''

''You know I *never* do interviews.''

Leona sighed into the phone. ''I'm afraid, cupcake, you don't have a choice this time.''

''What do you mean, this time?''

"Your new contract with the syndicate," Leona explained, "says you'll do whatever interviews they request, and for the first time, they've insisted on this one."

The beginnings of a headache blossomed behind Devon's eyes. "And if I refuse?"

Leona's sharp intake of breath hissed in her ear. "They'll void your contract and sue you for everything you're worth."

"Which isn't much," Devon said with a sharp laugh. Her syndicate salary was her only income, and she barely managed to pay her bills. She couldn't have afforded her house without Aunt Bessie's bequest as the modest down payment.

"Besides," Leona said, "I keep trying to tell you, the only way to survive in today's market is to go multimedia. You've got to take the plunge sometime. Why not make it big on Sara's show?"

Devon gulped. "But a whole hour. What will I talk about?"

"Babies and cooking, what else?" A long silence filled the other end of the line before Leona spoke again. "There is a slight hitch."

"Don't tell me I have to come to New York."

Colin raised his head from diapering Amanda on the sofa and looked at her with interest. Diaper pins sprouted between his lips. She turned her back on his curiosity.

"No need to come here," Leona said. "Sara will bring her show to Florida. I told her about your renovations. She wants to film next month at your house."

"Next month! The house won't be ready for six months, maybe more. My contractor's in the hospital."

"Don't worry about the house. Sara wants to see the project in progress, but there is another problem."

Devon's stomach knotted. It had to be bad news, and between Mike's incident, Amanda's arrival and the syndicate contract, she'd had enough bad news to last a year. "What problem?"

"She wants the interview to include your husband and baby."

"Are you crazy?" Devon sputtered softly into the phone, hoping Colin wouldn't hear. "You know I don't have a husband and baby. I made them up out of thin air for my column. What did you tell her?"

"What could I tell her without blowing your image? I told her *yes*. Your five-year refusal to make public appearances has everyone clamoring to know more about you, driving your asking price through the roof. Even if the syndicate hadn't insisted, the money is too good to turn down." She named a six-figure sum that took Devon's breath away.

Devon glanced back toward Colin, who had changed Amanda and now held her securely in one arm as he deftly popped the top on a can of formula, filled a bottle and settled back into the rocker to feed her. The baby's tiny sucking noises sounded all the way across the room. The kitchen's snug atmosphere, the big man cradling the child in his powerful arms and the desperation of her own situation gave rise to a brainstorm.

"I have an idea, Leona, but it will take time to work it out. I'll get back to you."

"I know you, Devon—"

"No, this time I promise—"

"You'll turn on your answering machine and ignore my calls until Sara's deadline passes. I'm catching the next flight to Tampa and bringing the contract with me. See you this evening."

"Leona, wait—"

Dead air filled her ear, and her mind churned. Across the room, Amanda kneaded Colin's big hand with her tiny fingers as he held her bottle.

The sight strengthened Devon's resolve. If she had to endure the interview, at least it would be for a good cause. She'd use her proceeds to hire a lawyer, one who could free her from Farnsworth's blackmail threats so she could put Amanda up for adoption. The kid deserved a home with a mother and father who loved her, not someone too terrified to touch her, not a scatterbrained, single writer who often forgot to feed herself, much less a baby. But first she'd need Colin's help.

She crossed the room and stood before him. Her idea was risky, but worth a try. Her heart thundered in her chest, and her palms were slick with perspiration.

He raised his head, shifting his attention from the child to her. "I didn't mean to eavesdrop, but I couldn't help hearing. Is there a problem?"

"That depends on you."

"Me?" His expression turned wary.

"Are you married?"

A frown pulled down the corners of his mouth. "Not anymore."

Why did he have to be so damned attractive? The strong line of his jaw, the way his tanned skin crinkled around his eyes when he smiled, the indentation in his chin the size of her little finger all distracted her. Her mouth went dry as she considered what to say. She hoped he wouldn't take her suggestion the wrong way.

She squared her shoulders, drew a deep breath and looked him straight in his misty gray eyes. "Colin O'Reilly, will you be my husband?"

Chapter Two

A baby's needs are simple: a safe, comfortable
crib, dry clothes, digestible food, and love.
Amanda Donovan, *Bringing Up Baby*

Her proposal caught him by surprise. Colin stopped
rocking and stared at her. "I'd be flattered by your
offer, except for the sneaking suspicion you're looking for a live-in baby-sitter, not a husband."

Devon clenched her hands in front of her, spread
them wide, opened her mouth as if to say something,
then dropped her hands to her sides. A pink flush
suffused her flawless skin. The woman might be as
crazy as a loon, but she was still damned pretty.

"I take it that's a no?" she finally blurted.

"Damn straight it's a no." He shifted Amanda's
weight on his arm and raised the bottle to prevent her
swallowing air. "I just divorced a woman that I loved
when I married her. I don't love you—I don't even
know you."

"But it's not—"

Memories of Felicia fired his temper. "You women are all alike, manipulating a man to serve your own purposes. Well, *this* man's had enough. I—"

"Will you be quiet and let me explain!" She hovered over him, her face within inches of his.

He forced himself to think with his head instead of his heart. All women weren't like Felicia. Where Felicia had been polished and calculating, Devon appeared casual and honest. Where Felicia had decorated their home in sterile, high-tech chrome and glass, Devon had created an atmosphere of warmth and comfort. Where Felicia would have refused to allow a baby in her house, regardless of the circumstances, Devon had opened her admittedly awkward arms to the child. No, Devon Clarke was definitely not Felicia.

For a moment, he forgot his anger. He breathed in the scent of sunshine mixed with a hint of jasmine in her hair. Her soft lips parted, revealing even white teeth.

"I'll listen," he said, knowing further involvement would be a mistake, "but the answer is still *no.*"

Her hazel eyes narrowed, and she straightened and glared at him with her hands on her hips. "My proposal is strictly a business proposition."

"Business? Then why don't you just *hire* a baby-sitter?"

"And why don't you stop jumping to conclusions?"

At the snap in her voice, the baby, now asleep, flinched in his arms. He set the bottle aside. "Do you have a crib?"

She flung up her hands and collapsed onto the sofa. "The baby furniture doesn't arrive until later today."

"The carrier will do. I want to put this little one to bed before we finish our discussion."

She rose from the sofa and returned with the car seat. He settled the sleeping baby in it, covered her with a blanket and lowered the carrier to the floor between the kitchen and family room.

Devon observed the child with a tremor that communicated her anxiety. "Will she be okay?"

He brushed a soft curl off the child's tiny forehead with his finger and wondered how Devon would deal with the infant when he was gone. "She's fine—for now."

He had no intention of becoming entangled in any way with Devon Clarke, except to finish her renovations as a favor to his dad, but she'd sparked his curiosity with her talk of marriage as a business proposition. When she'd settled back onto the sofa and crossed her trim ankles on the coffee table before her, he realized his curiosity wasn't the only part of him she'd aroused.

He sat back in the rocker, braced his work boots on the floor and challenged her. "Just what kind of business did you have in mind?"

"There's good money involved," she said.

"For baby-sitting? Give me a break."

"I told you, it's *not* babysitting. It's..." Her face crumpled into a frown that drew her delicate brows together as she struggled for words.

He wanted to smooth the worry wrinkles from the satin skin of her high forehead, but he denied his dangerous impulse and grasped the chair arms instead. "It's what?"

She raised her brows and forced a smile. "It's a television show."

"Whoa, that's it. I'm no actor." He climbed to his feet and strode toward the hallway. "Thanks for the coffee."

"Wait." She rushed after him and grabbed his arm. "You won't have to act, just be yourself."

"Then what does being your husband have to do with it?"

Her lips twisted in a wry expression. "It's a long story."

"Sorry, Devon." He fastened his tool belt and settled it on his hips. "I don't have time for long tales. I have work to do."

"Colin, please." Desperation filled her voice. "I'll split the money, fifty-fifty."

He shook his head and lifted her hand from his arm. "I don't think so. You'd better find another—" he almost let *sucker* slip "—candidate."

"Fine." The gold flecks in her eyes flashed with anger. "If you want to turn up your nose at $125,000, be my guest."

"Yeah…" Her words took a second to register. His jaw dropped. "Did you say $125,000?"

She folded her arms across small, firm breasts and smiled at him with a satisfied look. "That's your half."

A hundred and twenty-five thousand dollars sounded tempting. Felicia and her bloodsucking attorney had cleaned him out in the divorce settlement, and his dad's hospital bills would be astronomical. He'd be a fool to pass up that kind of money, and Mike O'Reilly hadn't raised a fool.

But only a fool would agree without first knowing all the details. "What do we have to do for a quarter million, take a flying leap off the Sunshine Skyway Bridge?"

"Nothing so drastic." She turned back toward the family room, confident now she had his full attention. "I'd better give you the background first."

He shed his tool belt once more and settled back into the rocker. "I'm all ears."

Not ears—she couldn't even see them beneath his thick hair—but angles of bone, curves of rippling muscles, taunting eyes and a broad mouth with a devilish grin. She'd never get anywhere looking at him.

She focused instead on the baby carrier and the child who needed a home. Even without the constrictions of her contract, obtaining funds for lawyers to protect Amanda Donovan's identity and insure Baby Amanda's adoption made her entire scheme necessary.

She straddled the hearth before the fireplace and rocked back and forth on the balls of her feet, trying to decide how to begin. "I'm a writer."

"So you said." He leaned back and crossed his arms over his chest, straining the fabric across his broad shoulders.

She jerked her gaze back to the baby. "I write a syndicated column, *Bringing Up Baby*."

"You?" He burst out with a half laugh, half snort. "Tell me another tall tale. Amanda Donovan is the Heloise of the baby world, but you? You can't even hold a baby, much less raise one."

"Look, I may not know beans about babies, but dozens of people write mysteries who've never committed a crime. Gramma Donovan was an expert on child care, and I use her journals for all my information." She scowled at him, daring him to laugh again.

His expression sobered. "You're serious, aren't you?"

She flopped into a chair opposite him. "I didn't set out to deceive anyone. I was still in junior college when Aunt Bessie died. We'd lived on her annuity, but that ended when she died, so I had to leave school and get a job."

She studied his expression, attempting to gauge his feelings, but his hooded eyes and the set of his jaw gave her no clues. She plunged ahead.

"Jake Blalock, the editor of the local paper, was looking for a general reporter who could also write a weekly family column. I was desperate for a job, so I agreed."

"And that's how *Bringing Up Baby* came about?"

She nodded. "I found Gramma Donovan's journals, fifteen years' worth from 1926 to 1944, among Aunt Bessie's papers. They were a gold mine. And I used her name because a few people in this town know me. My credibility as a family columnist would have been zilch.''

"And the column was a success.'' The toneless quality of his voice left her guessing about his opinion of her.

"Amazingly so. Within a few months, it was picked up by a national syndicate. Two years later, I converted Gramma's recipes into a cookbook, engaged Leona as my agent, and the rest, as they say, is history.''

His eyes widened. "So that's how you inherited the baby. Her parents had read your columns.''

Devon nodded. "I didn't know Amanda existed until the attorney appeared on my doorstep this morning. Now you see why I have to find a place for her—''

"Spare me.'' He reined in his temper. Devon Clarke had built herself a tidy, profitable career, with no place in her life for a family. He almost choked on her resemblance to Felicia. "Just tell me where I—as a husband—would fit into all this.''

Her eyes gleamed. "So you'll do it?''

"Where do I fit in, *if* I agree?''

She seemed to shrivel before his eyes like an inflatable pool toy with an air leak. "That was Leona on the phone. Sara Davis wants to spotlight Amanda Donovan at home in her next television special.''

He gave a low whistle. "Sara Davis? You're talking big time. Her show's been at the top of the ratings for almost three years now.''

She nodded. "She's asked that my husband and baby, whom she doesn't know are just inventions for the column, be included in the interview. My contract with the syndicate obligates me—and the money was too good to turn down.''

"Of course." He tried not to feel bitter. After all, acquiring money was his motivation, too. But he had an ailing father, a Mount Everest of medical bills and no bank account, while Devon Clarke appeared to have no shortage of ready cash, judging by her house and remodeling budget. He remembered how Felicia had insisted, "One can never be too rich or too thin." His former wife and the woman across from him could be soul sisters.

"Don't get me wrong," she said. "I only want the money for—"

"How you spend your money is none of my business. Just tell me what Mr. Amanda Donovan would have to do."

"Nothing you can't handle. Jeff—that's the name I gave him—is a contractor, a sort of Norm Abrams and Bob Vila rolled into one. That's why all you have to do is play yourself. Saw a few boards, hammer a few nails—"

"I've seen those interview shows," he said. "There's the obligatory sofa scene, wife snuggled at husband's side, holding hands and smiling at each other."

"We'll have a whole month to practice—" she colored, evidently realizing what she'd said "—I mean, to prepare for the charade."

"What about the house? I couldn't finish it in a month, even if Dad could help." He rose to his feet and headed toward the door. "You'd better find yourself another husband—and contractor. When Dad comes out of the hospital, he's going to need round-the-clock care. I can't do that and get much done here.''

She clutched his arm as he passed. ''I have an idea that might solve both our problems.''

He towered over her by a head, and her hand burned on his arm. He resisted the urge to run his fingers through her thick, strawberry blond curls and stepped away, breaking her grip on him. ''I don't know, lady. You come up with the craziest ideas I've ever heard.''

''This one isn't crazy. Come with me.'' She rushed up the hallway, and he followed her to the dining room where she stood, pirouetting on bare feet in the center of the spacious room. ''It's almost finished. Once the pocket doors are hung and the painting's completed, it would make a perfect bedroom for Mike, with easy access to the bath, kitchen and family room.''

''I don't know—''

''Sure, don't you see?'' she said. ''You and I could both work here and take care of Mike at the same time.''

''Did you learn nursing from those journals, too?'' he asked.

He regretted his sarcasm when sadness enveloped her. ''Aunt Bessie was bedridden for two years before she died, so I have lots of nursing experience.''

She seemed compassionate, but was her concern for his father genuine or just an added incentive to enroll him in her scheme? Once, he'd have trusted his instincts, but that was before he'd married Felicia, who had honed deception to a fine art.

Amanda's shrill cry saved him from making a decision.

The sound rooted Devon to the spot, and she turned eyes round with apprehension on him. "What do I do now?"

He sighed in exasperation. "You find out why she's crying, then fix whatever the problem is."

"But how?"

"Use your head. You wrote all those columns. Somewhere in that brain of yours is all the information you need. All you have to do is put it to use. Now if you'll excuse me, I have work to do." He picked up a tape and began measuring the unfinished door that stretched across the sawhorses.

Devon watched him while Amanda's cries accelerated, hoping Colin would give in and take charge of the baby. When he picked up the power saw and flicked the switch, she rushed back toward the kitchen.

The baby's face was red with rage, and Devon experienced a sharp stab of conscience at the child's discomfort. When she reached into the carrier, Amanda latched onto her finger with one delicate hand, and responsibility for the tiny bundle fate had dropped on her doorstep overpowered her. Would Amanda be content—or even safe—with such an incompetent parent?

She lifted the baby clumsily, laid her on a blanket on the sofa, slipped a finger beneath the child's plastic pants as she'd seen Colin do and quickly retracted it, covered with a brown, disgusting goo. She lunged for the baby wipes in the carryall to clean her finger.

She'd never changed a baby before, but she'd better learn. Even with the best of lawyers, it might be weeks before she found the right family and finalized adoption plans. Setting her mouth in a determined line and holding her breath against the smell, she eased off the dirty diaper and cleaned Amanda's tiny bottom with baby wipes.

The baby pumped her chubby legs and gurgled.

Devon cooed at her. "You're a pwetty widdle thing."

Amanda laughed, grabbed a fistful of Devon's T-shirt, kicked her fat little legs and wiggled. Devon's hands shook as she struggled to spear a pin into the clean diaper. What if she stuck the child?

After fastening the second pin, she tugged the plastic pants over the clean diaper while Amanda gurgled and smiled at her. Only then did she notice that the noise from the dining room had ceased. She glanced toward the hall. Colin was leaning against the door frame, watching her.

She flushed with embarrassment, wondering if he'd heard her babbling baby talk. Between her fear of caring for Amanda and the reaction of her body to Colin's enigmatic expression, Devon's senses flashed on overload. Good thing she'd just finished her column. It might take a week to concentrate on work again.

"Moving van's arrived," he said. "Where do you want Amanda's furniture?"

"Upstairs in my room. It's the only other habitable place in the house."

Colin nodded and disappeared down the hallway. Devon strapped Amanda in her carrier, set it on the floor where it wouldn't topple, washed her hands at the kitchen sink and hurried to the front porch to observe the unloading.

One by one, Colin and the driver wrestled a canopied spindle crib, rocking chair, bureau and changing table, all in sparkling white, up the porch steps, into the hall, up the stairs and into Devon's big, sunny bedroom at the front of the house.

"Where do you want the rest of it?" Colin asked.

"The rest?" She slumped against the porch column. "You've already carried in more furniture for the kid than I have in the whole house."

Colin pointed toward the van, where the driver continued to remove articles. "There's a portable crib, playpen, swing, high chair and stroller."

"Carry those into the family room." Devon watched in amazement as the men made several more trips into the house, stacked items in the hallway, then covered them with drop cloths against the dust. The last load included a small plastic pool, a baby's toilet seat, a life-size stuffed chimp and lion. Amanda even had her own computer and video-game library and a Mickey Mouse telephone.

"That oughta do it, lady," the driver said. "Sign here."

"The kid has enough stuff to open her own retail business." Devon scrawled her name across the form.

"You can always have a yard sale." The driver handed her a receipt, tossed the last of the moving blankets into the truck and drove off.

Across the street, an ancient green Buick pulled away from the curb and followed the van. The driver, a middle-aged man with a balding head, didn't look familiar.

"Something wrong?" Colin asked.

Devon shrugged. "Just a stranger. Neighborhood Watch tells us to keep an eye out."

Colin observed the battered Buick turn the corner. "Could be a new neighbor you haven't met—or a salesman."

"You're probably right." But she couldn't shake the apprehension she'd felt when the man's tiny porcine eyes locked briefly with hers.

She chalked up her fear as emotional residue from her roller-coaster day and followed Colin inside.

Chapter Three

> Being a mother is a twenty-four-hour job—with
> no time off for good behavior. Relaxing your
> vigilance for even an instant invites disaster.
> Amanda Donovan, *Bringing Up Baby*

Ernest Potts circled the block and once more drove slowly past the large Victorian house on Tangerine Street. Tailing the van all the way from Kansas City to Florida's west coast had frayed his nerves. When he'd almost lost it temporarily in Chattanooga and again outside Atlanta, he'd panicked because he'd been depending on the van's destination to reveal the identity of Amanda's guardian. His persistence had paid off. He made a mental note of the house number and pulled away.

Back in his room at the rundown motel on the outskirts of the business district, he extracted a beer from his foam cooler and reclined against the bed's headboard. His luck was beginning to change. He could feel it.

His luck had hit bottom thirty years ago when his mother divorced his father, married Chadwick Phillips and gave birth to his half brother, Chad. He'd battled for years to gain the attention and money his mother had lavished on his handsome younger brother. But not anymore. Mother was long dead, and before long, dear deceased Chad would be providing him with an income for life.

He reached for the phone and dialed long distance.

"Yeah?" Muriel's nasal voice answered.

"Pay dirt, sugar."

"You found her?"

"Movers led me straight to her. Now it's only a matter of time, and she's all ours."

"And the money?"

"Of course the money. That's the whole point." He pictured Muriel's sweet, sagging face beneath her bleached blond hair and heard her chewing gum pop over the wire.

"I still don't see how you're going to pull this off, Mr. Brilliant. Your half brother hated your guts and made it plenty clear what he thought of you looking after his kid."

Ernest Potts swigged his beer and wiped his mouth with the back of his hand. "You watch television, sugar. The courts are crazy these days to keep kids with their blood kin. All we gotta do is prove the couple are rotten parents."

"How're you gonna do that? They may be great with kids, for all you know."

Her whine was beginning to get on his nerves. "They can be the best parents in the world, but if the kid keeps having unfortunate accidents—or even disappears, no judge in his right mind will let them keep her, especially when her loving Uncle Ern and Aunt Muriel want her.''

''What are you gonna do?''

''Maybe it's better you don't know all the plans. That way you can play dumb if you're questioned.'' He grinned at himself in the dusty mirror above the bureau. Playing dumb was Muriel's strong suit.

''You won't hurt the kid, will you?''

''Not a chance.'' He laughed again. ''Wouldn't want to risk killing the goose that lays the golden eggs.''

He set down the receiver, plumped the pillows against the headboard and lay against them. If his scheme was to be successful, he had to make some very careful plans. But his fifteen-hundred-mile pursuit of the moving van caught up with him, and while he slept, dollar signs and trust funds danced in his dreams.

''YOU'VE BEEN FED and changed, so now what do you want?'' Devon eyed the screaming child with dismay as she knelt and dug into the carryall in search of a toy. Her hand closed around a plastic rattle. She dragged it out and shook it inches from the red, tear-streaked face.

The baby's cries ceased, and she reached out with chubby fingers wet with drool, grabbed the toy and shoved it into her mouth.

''Well,'' Devon mused, rocking back on her heels, ''that was easy enough. Maybe I'm getting the hang of this baby business.''

She'd no sooner risen to her feet than the rattle struck her ankle, and Amanda's cries resumed at full volume. Devon pulled out a clean toy, which Amanda clutched, then tossed onto the floor. A third toy met the same fate.

"Lord, give me strength." Devon scooped up the last toy with one hand and Amanda with the other and laid the wiggling body against her shoulder. The child snuggled against her, nuzzling her neck, and Devon fidgeted against the unaccustomed sensation. "You need a real home, kid. This is just a stopover on your way to someplace permanent, so don't expect the kind of attention you're used to."

She caressed the soft skin at the back of Amanda's head and twined her fingers through the fine, silky curls of blond hair. Poor kid. It was tough being an orphan.

Memories of her own solitary childhood strengthened her determination to place Amanda in a proper home, but first she'd need money for her legal battle, which meant enlisting Colin for the Davis interview. She had to convince him. She had no backup plan if he refused.

With Amanda balanced on her shoulder, she moved into the kitchen, dropped the toy into the sink to be washed and extracted a large aluminum dish from the freezer.

A well-fed man is a happy man, Gramma Donovan's journal entries vowed. Maybe with a good meal in his stomach, Colin would see things her way. She struggled to remove the cardboard cover marked

Paul's Greek Market and Deli, but the job required two hands.

"Sit here a minute, kid." She lowered Amanda to the gleaming tile floor, then pried the cover from the container. After popping the dish into the oven, she surveyed the contents of the refrigerator to plan the rest of her menu.

When she reached down to pick up Amanda, the baby was gone.

"Amanda?" A quick glance revealed the child was no longer in the kitchen. How could such a tiny body move that fast? "Come to Devon, kiddo."

She tore through the dining nook and family room, but found no sign of the baby. The door to the hallway stood open, and in the dust and debris on the floor, she spotted handprints and drag marks from tiny knees and toes.

Following the tracks, she skidded down the hall, bumping into baby furniture and tripping over toys, but the handprints disappeared among the chaos of footprints created by the movers when they'd brought in the furniture.

Devon turned into the dining room, where Colin was planing the edge of a paneled door.

"Have you seen her?" Panic edged her voice.

"The baby?" He raised the plane and seared her with a scathing look. "You turned her loose in this place? Are you out of your mind?"

She suppressed the urge to smack his handsome face. "I just set her down for a minute. I had no idea she could move so fast. So enough already with the accusations, just help me find her."

He dropped his tools and scoured the room, turning up drop cloths and checking behind lumber stacked against the wall. "We'd better find her fast. With the tacks and nails strewn across the floor—"

A crash, followed by a baby's shrill scream, resounded in the living room.

"Oh, Lord, she's hurt!" Devon bolted across the hall. Where earlier a board had spanned two ladders, a space gaped, and below it lay a jumble of canvas and paint cans.

Terror clutched at Devon's stomach. If one of those cans had hit the child... She fell to her knees in a puddle of Moonglow Yellow and began working her way through the debris toward the fallen objects.

Colin thrust past her, tossed the heavy cans aside and flung back the canvas. Amanda's brown eyes blinked in the light, and at the sight of Colin, her cries ceased. She raised her arms to him and gurgled. With a muffled cry, he gathered up the child and began checking her for injuries.

Watching the powerful man's gentle handling of the child created a strange prickling behind Devon's eyelids, and she blinked away tears. "Is she okay?"

"No thanks to you," he grated out between clenched teeth. "She must have pulled the canvas and brought down the board and paint cans, but somehow they all missed her."

Devon felt the blood leave her face. "I only took my eyes off her for a minute—"

"This baby's life is in your hands." He glowered at her over the head of golden curls. "If you screw up big time, she doesn't get a second chance."

She took Amanda from him and cradled her against her chest. "Thanks—"

Before she could express her gratitude, he'd turned his back and returned to the dining room.

COLIN STRUGGLED TO COOL his temper and focus on his work, but once his anger had faded, his stomach began to rumble like a power sander. He'd missed supper the night before when he'd taken his father to the hospital, this morning he'd come straight from the hospital to work, and he'd used his lunch break to visit his dad. His only nourishment had been coffee and a couple of Devon's cookies. Now the aroma of garlic and tomato sauce drifted through the sawdust-filled room, making his mouth water.

Between the hunger pains and the proposition Devon had offered him, he couldn't concentrate. Measure twice, cut once, his dad had always told him. Hell, he'd measured the door five damn times already and he still couldn't remember the dimensions.

He retracted his tape measure, shoved his pencil behind his ear and resisted the urge to slip down the hallway for another peek at Devon and the baby. From the anguish on her face at Amanda's near tragedy, he doubted she'd let the child out of her sight again soon. Even though she handled the baby clumsily with panic written all over her lovely face, watching the two of them together evoked strange feelings in him, dangerous emotions that encouraged him to accept her offer to pose as her husband.

He tossed the tape measure into the toolbox with disgust. Involvement with another career-minded female was the last thing he needed. It had taken two years, three attorneys and all his savings to disentangle him from Felicia. He'd be crazy to allow himself within ten feet of another like her, much less consider moving in with one, even for his father's sake.

"Would you like to stay for supper? I made plenty." Devon stood in the doorway, juggling Amanda on her shoulder. She'd scrubbed the paint from her knees and changed into a flowered dress with a short divided skirt that emphasized her long legs. A hint of makeup amplified the emerald in her eyes. Amanda drooled over her shoulder, soaking the floral fabric.

"You need a towel," he warned.

"What?"

"She's drooling all over you."

He stepped into the family room, retrieved a diaper from the carryall and returned to tuck it across Devon's shoulder. The fresh scent of baby powder and jasmine filled his nostrils, and the warmth of Devon's skin against his relayed pleasure signals to his groin.

"Thanks." She smiled up at him. "Now, how about some supper?"

"I don't—" Before he could decline, the doorbell chimed.

"Would you hold her a minute?" Without waiting for an answer, she passed Amanda to him and hurried to the door.

"Devon, you look marvelous!" A short, plump woman in a fire-engine red dress whisked in like a whirlwind and threw her arms around Devon. "It's wonderful to see you, but this humid Florida climate—it's worse than New York in summer, which is hotter than Hades."

"You're just in time for supper," Devon said. She closed the door behind the woman and turned to him. "Colin O'Reilly and Amanda, meet Leona Wiggins, my agent."

The little woman's dark eyes sparkled. "Delighted, Mr. O'Reilly. Devon, you do work fast. A husband and baby conjured up in less than eight hours. I am impressed."

"I'm not—" Colin began, but Amanda cut loose an earsplitting shriek. He checked her diaper. "Excuse me, I'll take care of her."

Devon watched him head toward the family room, crooning in the baby's ear as he went, and turned to catch Leona studying them.

"That's a great package," Leona said. "A handsome hunk who loves kids and an adorable baby. They'll knock the socks off Sara Davis."

"Nothing's final yet," Devon said. "Come have something to eat, and we'll talk."

In the family room, Colin spread a blanket, then laid Amanda on the sofa and removed her plastic pants and wet diaper. "I didn't know anybody still used cloth diapers these days," he grumbled.

"According to Amanda Donovan," Leona said, "disposable diapers are an environmental disaster. She advocates cloth diapers only, dried in the sunshine."

Colin passed the wet diaper to Devon, who took it with a grimace, holding it at arm's length.

"I have a feeling," he said, "that after washing a few loads of these, Mrs. Donovan may have a change of heart."

Leona grinned at him, then fixed Devon with a knowing smile. "I'd say she's already had a change of heart."

"Leona!" Heat crept across Devon's face.

When she returned from depositing the diaper in the pail in the laundry room, Leona sat ensconced on the sofa with Amanda gurgling and cooing on her lap, and Colin leaning over her shoulder, making faces at the child.

While she worked the cork from a bottle of Chianti, Devon studied the picture they made, Leona looking like a doting grandma and Colin a proud father. His natural ease with the baby alleviated some of her own terror. Why hadn't a man with such an obvious love of children settled down and produced a houseful of his own kids years ago?

She poured the wine, then removed the casserole from the oven. "Come and get it."

Amanda's eyelids sagged with sleep as Leona settled her in the carrier and set it near the table.

Colin straightened and shoved his hands into his back pockets. "Sorry, but I promised Dad—"

"You have to eat," Devon said. "Mike wouldn't want you to neglect your health for his sake. And after all the help you've given me today, feeding you is the least I can do."

Colin gazed at her flushed cheeks above the steaming dish. A perfect image of Little Susie Homemaker. But a homemaker who wanted to be rid of Amanda as soon as the child had played its part in furthering her career.

His head told his feet to make tracks, but his stomach, enticed by the aroma of cheese and garlic bread, directed him toward the table, where he pulled out a chair for Leona.

"Smells heavenly," Leona said. "What is it?"

"*Pastitio,*" Devon replied. "Greek lasagna."

Colin accepted the heaping plate she handed him. "Another of Gramma Donovan's recipes?"

She detected a trace of bitterness in his voice and wondered how she'd antagonized him. She hid her hurt feelings with a smile. "No, it's made in a deli in Tarpon Springs."

"Wherever you found it," Leona said, "it's delicious. The food on the plane was abominable as usual, and I'm starved." She demolished two servings while she maintained a running commentary on the latest Broadway shows.

Devon kept her guests well supplied with food and drink, all the while aware of the restive disposition of the big man across from her. She racked her brain, trying to pinpoint what she had done to upset him, and concluded that concern for his father was causing his edgy behavior.

When Devon had cleared the plates and served coffee, Leona brought her attaché case to the table. "Time to get down to work."

Colin laid his napkin aside and stood. "And time for me to leave."

"Don't be silly, Mr. O'Reilly," Leona said. "This concerns you, too."

"I haven't decided whether to accept Devon's proposition." The coolness in his eyes made Devon shiver.

Leona clutched his arm and tugged him down into his chair. "All the more reason for you to stay, so you'll know the facts."

Devon stirred her coffee and avoided his piercing glance. "What's the deal, Leona?"

"A quarter million for a one-hour interview, to be filmed in thirty days."

Devon frowned. "I thought you said it was a Christmas special."

Leona patted her hand. "Quite right. They'll need a couple of months to edit and complete the sound track, then the show will air in early December."

"That seems simple enough," Devon said. "I just take Sara on a tour of the house, answer a few questions, introduce her to my husband and baby—and that's it?"

"Not exactly." Leona dug into her case and withdrew a sheaf of papers. "Sara asked for a few specifics."

"Like what?" Devon's glance flew to Colin's face, but his stony expression didn't waver.

"You'll need to decorate as if for Christmas," Leona said.

Devon nodded. "That's easy enough."

"There's more." Leona handed her a clipping. "Remember the column you wrote about your wedding on the beach at sunset? It was one of Sara's favorites. She's asked to use footage from the videotapes."

Devon dropped the clipping. "What videotapes?"

"From the ceremony." Leona shuffled through the contents of her case and extracted a pen.

"But there *was* no ceremony!"

A muscle twitched in Colin's jaw, and Devon couldn't tell if he was angry or amused. He crossed his forearms on the table and leaned toward her. "'O what a tangled web—'"

"No need to throw quotes at me," she snapped. "I know the predicament I'm in."

"Relax, both of you," Leona said. "All these problems can be worked out. But first, how much did you offer Colin?"

"Half."

"Half?" Leona's voice cracked. "Are you sure that's a good idea?"

Devon locked her gaze with the cold steel of Colin's eyes. She didn't want him doing her any favors. "Half, or the whole deal's off."

Leona heaved a sigh of resignation. "That certainly makes divvying up easier. For that kind of money, Colin, you shouldn't mind."

"I haven't accepted yet." His tone revealed none of his feelings.

"Of course you'll accept," Leona said with a smile. "How could you turn down that much money for a few weeks' work?"

"On principle?" Colin returned her smile with a grin that never reached his eyes.

"Nonsense," Leona said. "It's like an acting job—neither immoral nor illegal. Especially once you're married."

"What!" Devon dropped her cup into its saucer, splashing coffee over the linen cloth. "That wasn't part of the deal."

"I'm outta here." Colin started to rise, but Leona restrained him with a manicured hand.

"It's very simple," she said. "We stage the seaside ceremony, based on the account in Amanda Donovan's column, and videotape it. You two remain married, in name only, of course, until after the show airs, then quietly have the marriage annulled. That solves two problems. It gives us the needed tape footage and makes lies about your marital status unnecessary."

"You must think I'm an idiot, Ms. Wiggins." Colin's low voice barely concealed his anger. "Even if I agreed to this crazy deal, the legal fees alone would eat all my profits. I've been down that road before."

"Not to worry." Leona dismissed his objection with a wave of her hand. "I guess Devon didn't tell you I'm also an attorney. I'll handle all the legal work as part of my regular commission."

"I don't know, Leona." Devon, too dazed to move, stared at the coffee stain spreading over the table-cloth. "This is getting more complicated than I'd anticipated."

"You can't pass up this opportunity," she said. "The name recognition, the money—it's the chance of a lifetime."

The money. Devon glanced over at Amanda, sleeping peacefully in her carrier. An orphan, just as she had been. And although Aunt Bessie had loved and cared for her, she'd always longed to be part of a family with a mother and father, brothers and sisters. The income from the Davis show was her only hope for securing that kind of life for the little surprise bundle Farnsworth had virtually left on her doorstep.

"You're right, Leona," she said. "I can't pass this up."

Disgust flickered across Colin's face. "I never thought you would. It's too important to your career."

"I tried to tell you—"

Leona cut her off before she could finish. "What about you, Colin? Are you in?"

He shook his head. "I just escaped one loveless marriage. I can't think of any reason, not even 125,000 big ones, to dive into another."

"Don't make up your mind now," Leona said. "Think it over tonight."

"Time isn't going to change my mind." He shoved back his chair and rose to his feet. "Thanks for supper, Devon. I'll be here bright and early tomorrow to finish the dining room."

Devon's hopes plummeted at his refusal. She tried to convince herself her disappointment wasn't personal. After all, the offer was only business.

She walked him to the door. "Thanks for your help with Amanda today. I'm such a klutz, and the kid deserves better. I'm glad she had you."

The icy granite of his eyes softened. "She's a sweetheart."

"Give my love to Mike. Tell him I'll visit when he's feeling better." She closed the door behind him and folded her arms across her stomach, which had tumbled like an Olympic gymnast since Leona's mention of marriage.

When she returned to the kitchen, Leona was loading the dishwasher. "Colin O'Reilly is perfection."

Devon shook her head. "We'd better look somewhere else, maybe the Actors' Guild. I don't think Colin will go for the idea."

"Don't be silly." Leona wiped her hands on a dish towel and studied her with twinkling eyes. "I saw the way he looked at you. He'll agree, all right."

Devon remembered Colin's sullen demeanor. "Are you sure we were watching the same man? He looked disgusted to me."

"Trust me, cupcake." Leona linked her arm through Devon's and led her toward the family room. "I know what I saw. Now I need the rest of the story."

"The rest?"

Leona pointed to Amanda. "How did you come by this little angel?"

"You're not going to believe it. You'd better sit down."

TWO HOURS LATER, Devon walked Leona to her rental car and gave her directions to her hotel on the beach. Had it been only this morning that her life had been so calm, uncluttered and uncomplicated?

Inside, she secured the locks and turned out the downstairs lights. Afraid she'd awaken the sleeping child if she lifted her out of the carrier, or worse, drop her on the stairs, she grabbed the carrier and toted it upstairs to her bedroom.

The crib with fresh linens stood in the corner, but Devon gauged the distance between it and her own bed with trepidation. What if Amanda cried in the night, and she didn't hear her? She gazed down at the child, lying still—too still.

She eased the carrier onto her bed and searched through her dresser drawer, scattering its contents in her haste to locate a small mirror. When she held the glass to the baby's face, breath fogged the glass, and she sagged with relief.

She stripped off her clothes, tugged on an oversize T-shirt, placed the carrier on the pillow beside her and lay down, holding her breath for fear she wouldn't hear Amanda's cries.

Exhaustion finally conquered anxiety, and she dropped off to sleep.

ERNIE POTTS STOLE into the shadows of the back porch, extracted the pick from his pocket and slipped it into the lock. A dog in the adjoining yard barked, and he froze. When no lights came on next door, he continued, teasing the lock until it clicked open.

He turned the knob and held his breath. If the house had an alarm system, he'd have to beat a fast retreat. The only thing worse than a blaring alarm would be a face-to-face confrontation with the man who'd helped the movers unload. Ernie was a big man, but that guy had been a helluva lot bigger. He stepped across the threshold and waited. Nothing happened. No alarm, no muscle man to block his way.

Moonlight streaming through the window over the sink lighted his route to the stove. He switched on the large front burner, extracted a saucepan from a nearby cabinet, then placed it on the element. From his jacket pocket, he pulled out a plastic bag and dumped its contents into the pot. He withdrew his cigarette lighter, held its flame to an oiled rag and dropped it into the pot. He waited for a few minutes until the contents caught fire, then scurried out the door.

As he crossed the backyard and headed for his car, parked on the next block, the beep of a smoke alarm blared in the old Victorian house.

Chapter Four

Every baby needs a secure and familiar environment in which to learn and grow.

Amanda Donovan, *Bringing Up Baby*

Mike O'Reilly was the last patient on Dr. Pete Packard's evening rounds. The doctor removed his stethoscope from his ears and fixed him with a puzzled stare. "We've been friends for a long time—"

"Thirty-five years," Mike said with a nod, "since before Colin was born."

"So I'm going to give it to you straight." He lowered his rotund frame to the bedside chair. "There's not a damn thing wrong with you. You're as healthy as a horse."

Mike's blue eyes twinkled. "I know."

"You know? You've let me run every test in the book on you, and you *know* you're healthy? Maybe I missed the most important test of all—a psychiatric exam."

Mike pulled himself into a sitting position and plumped the pillows behind him. "There's nothing wrong with my mind, except that I'm worried about Colin. I'll need your help, Pete."

"Colin's not ill, is he?"

Mike tapped the blue hospital gown over his chest. "He's sick at heart."

"His divorce?"

"He's lost his center, his focus in life. Oh, I don't blame Felicia. She was too young when they married, didn't know what she wanted. Unfortunately, when she figured out what was important to her, it didn't include Colin or the family he longs for."

Pete leaned back and tapped his lips with his forefinger. "I'm just an old general practitioner, so you'll have to explain how your playing invalid is going to make Colin happy. On the contrary, you're probably worrying him to death."

Mike rubbed his hands together and grinned. "It's the best plan—and the most fun—I've had since before Katie died."

Pete leaned toward the bed for Mike's explanation.

A half hour later, he walked toward the door. "If the Board of Medical Ethics finds out I have any part in this, they'll have my license."

"Like I said," Mike insisted, "my plan isn't harming anyone, and it could make several people happy, including me."

"I hope you're right. Colin's not going to like his dad scaring him half to death—or meddling in his love life."

"You just keep your end of the bargain and leave Colin to me." Mike reached for the television remote control. "And, Pete..."

"Yes?"

"Thanks. It may not be what you had in mind, but you've done my heart a world of good."

"You're a sentimental old coot." Pete rammed his stethoscope into the pocket of his white coat and left the room.

COLIN STOPPED at the nurses' station of the cardiac wing. "I know it's past visiting hours, but may I see Mike O'Reilly?"

The gray-haired nurse, who looked as if her feet hurt, flipped open a chart. "Are you his son?"

He nodded.

"Dr. Packard's left instructions that you can see your father anytime."

Fear for his father gripped him with a vengeance. "How is he?"

"He's resting as comfortably as can be expected," she said with a professional smile.

Unconvinced, he strode down the tiled hallway to his father's room. The old man lay propped against his pillows with his eyes shut. Colin reached across him for the remote and turned off the television.

His father opened his eyes. "I thought I heard your voice down the hall."

"How are you, Dad?" His stomach twisted with pain. His father had always been a vibrant, active man. Now, for the first time, lying so quiet and still in the hospital bed, he seemed old.

He struggled to sit upright, and Colin placed an arm around his shoulders to help him up. He lay still for a moment, as if the effort had worn him out.

"I'm fine," he said in a weak voice that Colin had to lean forward to hear.

"And what did Dr. Pete have to say?"

His father flipped his hand back and forth in a so-so gesture. "He says as long as I get plenty of bed rest and don't get too excited, I should be okay."

Colin's heart sank. Bed rest was like a death sentence to a man as energetic as his dad had always been.

"Let's not talk about me," his father said in a stronger voice. "Tell me how you like working for Devon Clarke."

Colin gave a half snort, half laugh. "The woman is crazy and the house is a zoo."

"Not anything you can't handle?" Some of the old sparkle returned to his father's eyes.

"The construction work?" Colin shook his head, exorcising intriguing thoughts of Devon Clarke in his arms. "But don't you think we should let someone else take over the job so I can look after you?"

"No!" The old man lay back, closed his eyes and clutched his chest.

Colin bent over him with alarm. "Dad, are you okay? Should I call the nurse?"

Mike grabbed the front of Colin's shirt, pulled him close and spoke in a strangled whisper. "That girl is like one of my own daughters. Don't abandon her now when she needs you."

"She doesn't need me. Any carpenter can finish what you started," Colin protested, but he couldn't erase from his mind the picture of Devon's red-gold curls bowed over Baby Amanda's blond ones. Or the flash of her hazel eyes and the delicate curve of her cheeks. She had the courage to face new situations without falling apart and, in fact, thought faster on her feet than any man he knew. The woman had embedded herself in his consciousness and wouldn't let go. The less he saw of her, the better.

His father winced and clutched his chest again. "She's all alone in the world and needs looking after. Promise me."

He had agitated his father, exactly what Dr. Pete had warned against. "Sure, Dad, don't worry. I promise."

The old man raised his hand from his chest and patted Colin's cheek. "You're a good boy, son. I love you."

"I love you, too, Dad." He had planned to tell him about the baby and Devon's offer for the television interview, but the old man had experienced enough excitement for one night. Colin sat quietly beside the bed until his father drifted off to sleep.

WHEN HE PULLED OUT of the hospital parking lot, his promise to his dad echoed in his mind. Because it meant so much to the old man, he'd agreed, against his better instincts, to continue working for Devon Clarke. He chuckled at his father's notion that she needed looking after. With her enterprising and manipulating mind, she'd do just fine on her own. He was the one who'd need to be cautious, or she'd soon have him sucked into her money-making schemes.

Instead of turning left toward his dad's house, he took a right and headed back to Devon's. As little as he relished the responsibility of watching out for her, a promise was a promise, and he wondered how the novice mother was faring with Amanda. She was in for one rough ride.

He turned down Devon's street and had almost reached her house when he spotted clouds of thick black smoke billowing out of the downstairs windows of the old Victorian.

He gunned the pickup truck the last hundred feet to the front of the house, braked against the curb and raced to the front door.

"Devon, wake up!" He pounded on the locked door and listened for sounds of life, but the only noise inside the house was the incessant beep of a smoke alarm.

He shrugged off his shirt, wrapped it around his arm and drew back, prepared to break the beveled glass of the door to gain entry.

"We're up here." Devon's voice floated down to him.

He bounded off the porch and glanced up, straining to see through the smoke-shrouded darkness. An acrid stench filled his nostrils and seared his lungs, and he coughed, gasping for air. Above him, the faint glow of a streetlight illuminated Devon, crouched on the porch roof outside her open bedroom window with Amanda's carrier crushed against her chest.

Fear for Devon and the child threatened to paralyze him. Between the dry tinder of the frame structure and dozens of cans of flammable paint stacked inside, the whole house could explode any second, tumbling them into an inferno below.

"Wait right there!" He hurtled down the walk toward his truck, ignoring the agony in his chest as he sucked in the smoke-laden air.

"We haven't much choice," Devon called after him with a nervous hiccup in her voice.

He dragged the expandable ladder from the truck bed, hefted it on his shoulder and raced back up the lawn toward the porch. Sirens sounded in the distance, increasing in volume as the fire trucks approached, but they were too far away to save Devon and Amanda if the porch caught fire.

He threw the ladder on the ground, extended it to its full length, then secured the catches before raising it to the eaves along the porch and clambering up. Devon's wide eyes glittered darkly in her pale face when he met her face-to-face at the roof's edge.

"Here—" she thrust the carrier toward him "—take the baby."

"I'll be back for you." Tucking the carrier under one arm, he began the precarious one-handed descent.

"I can take care of myself," she insisted, and swung a leg onto the ladder.

The flash of a firm, round buttock beneath the hem of her shirt almost caused him to lose his grip on the rung, and he averted his eyes toward the ground. Amanda cooed and chuckled in his arm as if the entire episode was some kind of lark, planned solely for her amusement.

A tanker and hook-and-ladder truck roared to a stop against the curb, and fire fighters began laying hose to the corner hydrant. An official approached just as Devon stepped off the ladder to the safety of the front lawn.

"Anyone else inside?" he asked.

Devon shook her head. "Thanks to Colin here."

The fire chief acknowledged Colin with a nod and returned his attention to Devon. "Any idea how or where the fire started?"

"I was asleep upstairs when the smoke alarm went off." She reached into the carryall slung over her shoulder and extracted her portable phone. "The halls were filled with smoke, so I grabbed the baby and the phone, crawled onto the porch roof and called 911."

Colin experienced a stab of sympathy for her when he saw tears flooding her eyes as she observed the clouds of foul smoke seeping out around the door-jambs and window casements.

He placed a consoling arm around her shoulders and pulled her against him. "Let's get out of the way so the fire fighters can do their job."

With the baby under his other arm, he led Devon across the lawn to his truck, opened the door and boosted her inside. She appeared small and fragile sitting alone on the wide seat, shivering and trying to catch her breath. Despite the heat, she seemed chilled to the bone.

He handed her the baby, then retrieved the shirt he'd flung onto the lawn in his rush for the ladder. When he tucked the garment around her slender shoulders, tenderness toward her overwhelmed him. She'd remained calm and cool in a crisis, thinking clearly and reacting quickly to save herself and the child. And now, in spite of the fact her home was about to go up in flames, she hadn't succumbed to hysteria. Not like Felicia. His former wife had wept buckets over a hangnail.

As if to contradict his thoughts, Devon jumped from the truck, thrust the baby into his arms and sprinted up the walk toward the front door.

"Wait," he yelled, making Amanda howl in protest. He lowered the carrier to the curb, raced after Devon and caught her as she vaulted up the porch steps. "Are you crazy?" He dragged her down the walk, dodging hoses and equipment. "You *never* go back into a burning building."

"Let me go." She twisted in his arms, struggling for release. "I have to—"

He grabbed her shoulders and swiveled her to face him. "What's so damned important you'd risk your life for it? If you're insured, everything can be replaced."

"Not Gramma Donovan's journals." She kicked him in the shin.

Startled by the unexpected attack, he loosened his grip. She raced toward the steps, but a fire fighter blocked her way. "You can't go in there, ma'am."

"I have to!"

She tried to circumvent the forceful fireman, who seized her firmly by the elbow and led her back to Colin. "You could help us out by keeping your wife out of the way."

"She's not—"

"I'm not—"

They both spoke at once, but the fireman returned to his duties, ignoring their outbursts.

Colin scowled at her. "That was the dumbest stunt I've ever witnessed. Doesn't your life mean more to you than some stupid newspaper column?"

Fury etched her face, and she shivered in helpless frustration, her fists clenched at her side. She opened her mouth as if to reply, but an angry shriek from Amanda interrupted her.

"*There's* your responsibility," he shouted, pointing toward the child, "not some worthless bundle of paper."

The baby's tiny face contorted with rage, and her cries pierced the air above the rumble of the fire engines. With a chagrined look, Devon knelt before the child, unfastened her restraints and gathered her awkwardly in her arms. Looking dazed and lost and lovely, she sank to the curb, cradling the screaming baby against her chest.

His conscience attacked him when he remembered his promise to his father, and he dropped to the pavement beside her and took Amanda from her arms. As if sensing his need for quiet, the baby ceased her cries, snuggled into the hollow of his throat and, easing her fist into her mouth, began to suck contentedly.

"I'm sorry—" he began.

"No, you were right." She tilted her face toward him. Disordered curls framed her face, delicate pink tinged her cheeks, and her eyes were swirls of gold and green. Soot smudged the tip of her upturned nose. "I wasn't thinking straight."

His anger transformed into a deep molten heat of longing, and every protective urge he'd ever known coalesced into a desire to shield her from all harm. He shifted the baby to his other arm and drew Devon's trembling body against him. "You thought straight when it mattered. Both of you are safe, thanks to your quick response."

The warmth of her seared through his jeans, Amanda's body weighed comfortably against his bare chest, and he reveled in the closeness, the rightness of woman and child in his arms. A brusque voice broke his reverie.

"You the owners?" The fire chief stood before them with a blackened object in his hands.

"I am." Devon stood and tugged her shirt over her thighs. Her calm dignity generated a reluctant approval from Colin.

"The fire's out," the chief said, "and except for the cabinets above the stove, there's only smoke damage."

"The stove?" she said. "Was there some kind of electrical short?"

He shook his head. "A burner was left on high and this pot caught fire. Some kind of rubbery substance in it created all the smoke. What the hell were you cooking, lady? Snow tires?"

Her lips puckered with uncertainty. "I wasn't cooking."

"Is this your pot?" He thrust the blackened object toward her.

She shrugged. "It could be. Under all that soot, I can't tell."

"Either you're unbelievably careless, leaving your stove on and your back door unlatched, or—"

"What are you trying to say?" Colin demanded.

"Do you live here, too?" the chief asked.

"No, I've done some work here, but tonight I was just passing by."

"What I'm saying is that the owner here—"

"Devon Clarke," she said.

"Ms. Clarke," he amended, "is either negligent or this fire was set intentionally."

"Devon may be scatterbrained," Colin said, his anger over her carelessness flaring anew at the chief's accusations, "but she's no arsonist."

"Thanks for your ringing vote of support," she said in a voice laced with sarcasm before crumpling back onto the curb.

Behind her, fire fighters stripped off their protective clothing and breathing equipment and began loading hoses into the trucks.

"We'll secure the premises for the night," the chief said, "and the arson investigators will be around at first light. Do you have someplace to stay?"

Remembering his promise to his father, Colin spoke up. "I'll take care of her."

After a final questioning look, the chief walked away.

Devon straightened her back and shoulders and lifted her chin. "I can take care of myself."

"You have no clothes, no money, no credit cards," Colin countered.

"I'll stay with Leona on the beach," she said.

"And the baby?" He shifted Amanda in his arms.

"I have her carryall with diapers and clean clothes."

"What about food?"

"If they'll just let me in the house to get my wallet and keys..."

He gestured toward the front entrance where yellow warning tape sealed the door. "Until their investigation's complete, I doubt they'll let anybody in."

A group of curious neighbors had gathered on the opposite side of the street, and an elderly woman broke away from the crowd and approached. Her quick blue eyes took in Devon's skimpy attire, Colin and the baby.

"You're welcome to stay with me awhile, Devon," she offered. "I'm so sorry about your lovely house."

"Thanks, Mrs. Kaplan," Devon said. "I've already made arrangements, but I'd appreciate your keeping an eye on things here until I can move back in."

The old woman nodded and crossed the street to rejoin the curious throng. Colin eased the sleeping Amanda into her carrier and secured it in the truck cab with the seat belt.

Devon climbed in next to the car seat and pulled out her portable phone. "I'll call Leona and tell her we're coming."

He placed his hand over the slender fingers that gripped the phone and fought against the emotions her vulnerability triggered in him. "Dad's guest room has a crib for the grandkids when they visit, and we're only a few blocks from here—more convenient for you to supervise the cleanup than from all the way out on the beach."

Drawing her feathery brows together in a thoughtful frown, Devon observed the slumbering child and pondered a moment before conceding. "But only for Amanda's sake."

She leaned back against the headrest and closed her eyes. The stench of smoke from her hair and shirt permeated the truck, and she wondered if the tightness in her chest resulted from fumes or the frantic pounding of her heart at Colin's touch.

After the smoke alarm awakened her, she'd almost panicked when she'd opened the door to a dark, smoke-filled hallway. Even once she'd dragged the baby to the safety of the porch roof, she'd wondered whether help would arrive before the fire consumed them.

When Colin O'Reilly, his tanned chest gleaming golden in the streetlight, had appeared on her lawn, he'd been an answer to a prayer, but now he sat hunched over the steering wheel, glowering with anger—and no wonder. He considered her a senseless ninny who'd attempted to enter a burning building to save her career. He hadn't allowed her to explain that Gramma Donovan's notebooks were her only family tie, a precious heirloom that meant almost as much to her as life itself.

Even worse, he thought her careless enough to set her own house afire. How could he know it had been months since she'd used the cooktop? If meals couldn't be prepared in the microwave or a conventional oven, she changed the menu.

As for the unlocked back door, she had no explanation. Ever since she'd moved into the big house alone, she'd followed an unvarying ritual of checking every door before going to bed, and tonight had been no exception. A piercing chill racked her. Someone had picked her lock and set the fire. But who? And why?

Colin's deep baritone interrupted her musings. "You okay?"

She studied his strong profile, silhouetted by the headlights of passing cars, and shuddered at the thought of what might have happened if he hadn't come along. "Thanks to you. Your truck screeched to a halt in front of the house like the timely arrival of a guardian angel."

"God looks after fools and little children." His toneless voice gave no clue to his feelings, and he kept his gaze on the road.

The blaze of her temper chased her chill away. "I know which category Amanda falls into, but I object if you're calling me a fool."

He shrugged. "If the shoe fits—"

"I *didn't* leave the stove on, if that's what you mean."

"Then who did—the tooth fairy?"

"Why are you so smug?" Amanda jerked in her sleep at the volume of the query, and Devon lowered her voice. "Is it beyond the realm of possibility that someone broke into my house and set the fire?"

He flicked a glance toward her. "Do you have enemies?"

"Not that I know of."

"Disgruntled readers?"

She shook her head. "And even if I did, none of them knows my true identity."

"You've just proved my point." A self-satisfied smile deepened the cleft in his chin.

"Don't be ridiculous. People who start fires aren't wrapped real tight to begin with. Have you considered that the arsonist doesn't know me and picked my house at random?"

A solemn look replaced his smile. "You're right. Look, I'm sorry. I've just gone through a nasty divorce, and I tend to take my problems out on those around me."

When she glimpsed the pain beneath his curt behavior, she bit back an angry reply. He had saved her life and was offering her shelter, so he wasn't *all* bad. In fact, under different circumstances, he'd be downright appealing. If nothing else good came out of the fire, at least she'd be living close to him for a while. She'd use that time to convince him to do the Sara Davis interview.

She tugged his shirt tighter around her shoulders, all too aware of him across the breadth of the carrier on the bench seat. Over the smoky smell of her own clothes, the scent of musky after-shave and wood shavings teased her nostrils. Just her luck. She was moving in with a man who looked and smelled fabulous, acted like a hero, loved children—and thought she was the dumbest thing since pet rocks. Not to mention that he considered her a first-class fraud.

Colin turned the truck into the driveway of a two-story Dutch Colonial, and she observed his muscles tense when the movement of the vehicle slid her toward him. Without a word, he killed the engine and sprinted around the truck. With Amanda under one arm and the carryall over the other, he trudged up the front walk.

In her weariness, she struggled to place one foot before the other and somehow made it up the steps into the house. Colin continued down a wide hallway, and she followed.

At the far end of the house, he entered a room, switched on a light and pointed toward an open door. "The bath's through there. I'll put the baby to bed while you clean up."

Without protest, she stumbled into the bathroom, closed the door and stripped off Colin's shirt and her grimy top. Beneath the pounding pulse of hot water, she scrubbed the oily residue of smoke from her hair and body and struggled to stay awake. A few minutes later, swathed in towels, she entered the bedroom to find Colin nowhere in sight.

Another of his denim shirts, clean, soft and faded, lay on the pillow of the turned-down bed. His thoughtfulness brought a contented smile to her lips. "What, no chocolate? What kind of hotel is this?"

At the sound of her voice, Amanda murmured in the crib, and Devon tucked a blanket around her. She towel-dried her hair, shrugged into the fresh shirt and slid between the cool sheets. In minutes, she dropped into an exhausted sleep.

She dreamed she was running, trying to escape a faceless pursuer, but baby furniture and stacks of diapers barred her way. In the distance, a golden man with pewter eyes called to her, but she couldn't reach him. Suddenly, railroad tracks appeared beneath her feet, and the scream of an approaching engine bore down on her.

She bolted upright with her heart pumping, perspiration beading her face, while the engine's wails resounded in the strange surroundings. She groped for the bedside lamp, and soft light flooded the guest room.

Like the call of an advancing locomotive, Amanda bellowed from the crib in the corner.

Forcing her tired lids to stay open, Devon threw back the covers and stumbled to the crib. "Poor kid, you're the only one whose day's been worse than mine."

Amanda cried more loudly in response and scrunched her tiny face in anger until it glowed beet purple. She'd kicked off her covers, and her fists and feet thrashed the air.

Devon checked Amanda's diaper, but it was unsoiled. What now? She scooped the writhing infant into her arms and searched her memory for the column she had written on babies who wouldn't sleep. What had Gramma Donovan recommended?

She settled into a rocking chair beside the crib and jiggled Amanda in the crook of her arm. Although she rocked gently and tried singing a soothing lullaby, the child's fussing escalated and her face reddened until Devon feared the infant would break every blood vessel in her face.

"Sorry, kiddo," she muttered. "My singing has that effect on everybody."

In desperation, remembering Gramma's advice on teething babies, she gently forced a finger into Amanda's mouth and attempted to massage her gums. The baby crunched down on her finger like a vice, and Devon yelped and jerked her hand away. Her reaction provoked an even angrier response from the cranky child.

Frustrated, she rose to her feet, slung the baby over her shoulder and paced the floor. Amanda continued to shriek loudly enough to wake the dead, and Devon hoped her cries would roust Colin to come to her rescue.

Thank God her readers couldn't see her now. What an exposé for the tabloids: Baby Expert Stumped! Hasn't A Clue How To Quiet Screaming Child! Amanda Donovan Found Dead Of Exhaustion At Dawn!

The word *colic* bubbled up from her memory. Maybe that was the problem. The poor kid had lost her parents, lived a week in a strange environment, been dragged halfway across the country to another strange place, which then caught fire—enough chaos to give anyone a bellyache.

Or maybe she was just hungry. With chagrin, Devon recalled her column on recognizing the differences in a baby's cries and what each sound indicated. What a crock of garbage that had been.

Amanda's cries all sounded the same, only some were louder than others.

Where was Colin? A man would have to sleep like the dead not to be awakened by the racket Amanda was producing.

Devon deposited the bundle of rage in the middle of the double bed and scrounged through the carry-all for a clean bottle and a can of formula. Minutes later, she returned to the rocker with the child and encouraged her to stop squalling long enough to give her the bottle.

Alternately, Amanda sucked and whimpered. When her tears ceased, Devon set aside the bottle. She remembered that babies should be burped, but feared waking her again and continued rocking. The child felt unwieldy in her arms, as uncomfortable as her first encounter with a tennis racket had been until the pro had taught her the proper grip. Maybe she'd soon get it right, but if she didn't, no problem. The child wouldn't be with her long, because she was determined to place Amanda with a real family as soon as possible.

Fatigue seeped through her bones, and her eyelids closed. She was only dimly aware sometime later that someone was taking the baby away. Through a fog of exhaustion, it barely registered when someone lifted her in strong arms and tucked her into bed. When warm lips brushed her forehead, she knew she was dreaming.

She drifted back into a deep sleep, surrounded by the fragrance of after-shave and wood shavings.

Chapter Five

> The introduction of solid food into your baby's diet is an important event. Choosing healthy foods sets a pattern for life. However, *never* allow mealtime to become a battle between a demanding mother and a reluctant eater.
>
> Amanda Donovan, *Bringing Up Baby*

Devon dreamed of arms like tender steel, lifting her as if she were weightless, pressing her close to muscles like warm, pliant rock. With a wistful sigh, she snuggled deeper into her pillow, where the crackle of paper beneath her cheek awakened her. She opened her eyes to sunlight filtering through the flowered-chintz draperies of the O'Reilly guest room, pulled herself upright and retrieved a note crumpled on her pillow.

"Gone to check on Dad," Colin had written. "Back soon. Help yourself to breakfast."

When she tiptoed to the crib where Amanda still slept peacefully, she caught sight of herself in the dresser mirror. In the too-large shirt with her hair as disheveled as a fright wig, she resembled a poster child for Save the Children. She raked her fingers through the tangled mass without effect, then rummaged through the carryall until she found a tiny comb-and-brush set of pink plastic decorated with bunnies.

"Desperate times, kiddo," she whispered to the slumbering child. "We girls have to stick together and pool our resources."

After a quick wash, brushing her teeth with her finger and taming her hair with Amanda's tiny comb, she set out in search of the kitchen.

Sunlight poured into the spacious room at the back of the house. An immense oaken table with a well-scrubbed surface, a low shelf filled with toys, a high chair in the corner and a bulletin board covered with snapshots indicated the kitchen was the hub of O'Reilly family activities.

She poured herself a cup of coffee from the coffeemaker Colin had left on for her and studied the photographs. A family grouping featured Mike with his arm around a plump, pleasant woman with laughing eyes as they stood in the midst of their children. Devon recognized Colin's sisters and brothers from the clefts in their chins and their mother's smile.

A tall, reed-slim blonde in a designer suit of watered silk linked arms with Colin and appraised the camera with an ice blue gaze. The photo captured the cool haughtiness of the woman, and Devon shuddered. No wonder Colin resisted posing as her husband. After a wife like the one in the picture, he'd be stepping down from caviar to Spam.

All the other family shots showed Colin with a niece or nephew on his lap or in his arms. Almost hidden among the overlapping photos, she spotted a fading picture of a beaming teenage Colin in wrestling trunks, holding aloft a trophy. Another revealed Colin, looking much as he had when she'd first met him, in work clothes with his tool belt slung on his hips, posing with another man before the rough framework of a house under construction. The grinning man with large, prominent teeth looked familiar, and when she detected the Habitat For Humanity sign across the doorway behind them, she realized with a jolt that the weathered-looking carpenter shaking Colin's hand was former president Jimmy Carter.

But the family groups held her attention. The sense of love and belonging emanating from those happy faces was what she'd yearned for all her life, what she wanted for Baby Amanda that she, as a single mother, couldn't give her. Only with the money from the Sara Davis interview could she engage lawyers to fight Farnsworth and see that Amanda was placed in the home she deserved.

With renewed resolve, Devon removed a directory from the counter beneath the wall phone and looked up the number of Leona's hotel.

"Good morning," Leona greeted her. "Have you convinced your handsome handyman to submit to Sara's questions?"

"Not exactly. There's been a slight hitch." Devon described the fire and Colin's rescue. "So I'm at his house now, and without clothes—"

"My, my, you do work fast," Leona said with a throaty chuckle.

"Lucky for you you're beyond my reach," Devon said with a flush. "Colin was merely being kind. There's nothing between us."

"Of course not," Leona replied with an agreeableness that suggested just the opposite. "Now, what do you need?"

Arguing with her agent's assumption of a dalliance between her and Colin would be futile, so she addressed the problem at hand. "Could you stop by the mall and pick me up something to wear? I'll reimburse you."

"I love any excuse to shop." Leona scribbled down the sizes and Colin's address as Devon gave them to her. "Then I'll come straight there, and together we'll extract a commitment from the reluctant Colin. Sara insists you sign this contract for the interview today."

"Call Sara and tell her about the fire. Maybe she'll give us some leeway." A whimper from the guest bedroom interrupted her. "Gotta go. The baby's awake."

As soon as she dropped the receiver onto its cradle, Amanda's protest ceased. Devon used the reprieve to call her insurance agent, who promised to send a restoration crew to her house that morning.

"They're real pros," he assured her. "They'll have you moved back in within three days tops."

Before Devon had finished with the insurance man, Amanda's cries resumed with an intensity that allowed no further delays. Hoping to pacify her before she worked herself into another rage, Devon raced into the guest room. The baby stopped crying when she spotted Devon. Her wide eyes sparkled and her lips curved upward in a toothless grin as Devon changed her diaper.

The child needed a bath to cleanse away the stench of smoke, but Devon decided to feed her first. A search of the carryall revealed she'd used the last of the formula the night before. Amanda whimpered with hunger.

She slung the baby over her shoulder. The sudden sensation of moist warmth reminded her she'd forgotten Amanda's plastic pants. She returned the child to the crib and began the clumsy diapering process all over again.

Amanda howled at the added delay, and Devon hurried with her into the kitchen. "Hang on, kiddo. Maybe there's some formula here someplace."

A search of the kitchen failed to turn up infant formula, but she discovered oatmeal, applesauce and canned evaporated milk, ingredients straight out of Gramma Donovan's journals.

She pulled the high chair out from the corner, strapped the baby in and rolled up the too-long sleeves of Colin's work shirt. Amanda's chubby face crumpled with distress as Devon dumped water and oatmeal into a bowl and shoved it in the microwave.

"Never fear, kiddo," she assured the child with feigned calm. "It's Amanda Donovan to the rescue."

COLIN ENTERED THE HOUSE silently, not wanting to awaken his sleeping guests. He eased down the hallway to the open door of the guest room and noted the empty bed and crib at the same time he heard voices in the kitchen.

He paused, remembering how he had paced the hallway the night before while Amanda screamed. He'd mustered every ounce of self-restraint to keep from opening the door and offering help. Devon had to learn that if she allowed her natural instincts to guide her, she could handle Amanda herself. But those natural instincts had taken forever to kick in. He had slid to the floor, waiting, and had finally fallen asleep.

When he awakened, Amanda was quiet, but light still glinted beneath the door. Stiff from sleeping crouched against the baseboard, he rose and opened the door a crack. Like a blow beneath the belt, the sight before him drove the breath from his body. More beautiful than a Renaissance Madonna, Devon cradled the slumbering baby in her arms, while the bedside lamp cast a nimbus of light around her gilded curls. Her head tilted toward the child, and golden lashes curled across the silky pinkness of her cheek. The baby nestled against the curve of her breasts, visible through the thin fabric of his old work shirt, and the grace of Devon's slender legs, extended before her and crossed demurely at the ankles, sent his blood galloping.

He stood for what seemed like hours, drinking in the beauty before him like a thirsty man consumes water, until his conscience prodded him. Devon needed sleep, true rest in a real bed. He lifted Amanda and placed her in the crib, then gathered Devon in his arms.

She stirred and snuggled deeper in his embrace with a sigh. He froze where he stood, fearful he'd awakened her, afraid he'd succumb to the desire to lower his lips to her rosy ones and kiss her senseless. Then common sense washed over him like a cascade of icy rain. Why hadn't he left her asleep in the chair? She could take care of herself, and he'd already learned the hard way the pain that came from caring for a woman. He'd been a fool to risk that fleeting kiss, to feel the compelling warmth of her smooth forehead beneath his lips. The sensation had left him yearning for more, and only with difficulty had he quit her room and returned to his cold, lonely bed.

Standing in the doorway, remembering the night before, he struggled with the emotions that still battled within him until a piercing shriek and loud crash from the kitchen propelled him down the hall.

He stopped abruptly in the doorway, astonished by the scene before him. His mother's kitchen, always immaculate, looked like a war zone. Amanda, covered with a thick paste, sat in the high chair beside the kitchen table, pounding the tray with a spoon and giggling with delight. Milk poured from an overturned can and puddled on the tabletop, while the refrigerator door stood ajar. Globs of runny oatmeal covered the room like a shelling from heavy artillery.

"What the hell is going on in here?" he demanded.

With a gasp, Devon rose from behind the table with her hands filled with shards of oatmeal-coated glass. "Breakfast?"

"Where did you learn to cook—demolition school?"

He drew a deep breath to keep from laughing. Applesauce dripped from her hair and coated one feathery brow, cereal spotted her shirt, and her wide eyes reflected the vacant look of a shell-shock victim. She stared at him with a stunned expression that failed to register a response to his sarcasm.

"You have to teach the kid that breakfast is to be eaten, not annihilated." He pulled out a chair, wiped a blob of oatmeal from the seat and guided her to it.

"I had no idea it would be this hard," she muttered as she dropped the glass fragments on the table and rubbed her sticky hands on her shirt.

"A plastic bowl makes cleanup easier." He wet paper towels and began dabbing glass and cereal from the floor.

"Any other advice, Dr. Spock?" She spoke with more energy now, as if coming out of shock.

"Yeah, the baby needs a bath."

She groaned and laid her head on the table, seemingly oblivious to the puddle of milk beneath her cheek.

He tried to put himself in her place. He'd grown up observing his brothers and sisters learning to eat solid food, but for someone who'd never experienced the messy and chaotic process, the first time could be traumatic. His memories induced sympathy. "Did *you* have any breakfast?"

Her only reply was a swift shake of her head that created eddies in the spilt milk.

He placed his hand on her shoulder and felt the warmth of her fragile body pulse beneath his palm. "Get yourself cleaned up. I'll tackle this mess and fix us both some breakfast."

She lifted her head and pushed her hair off her forehead. Warmth flashed in her eyes and her lips lifted in a half smile. "Thanks."

Memories of her in his arms almost convinced him to reach out for her and kiss her again. He quelled his rebellious impulses and gritted his teeth. "My robe is hanging in the upstairs bathroom. That'll have to do until we figure out what to do about your clothes."

She smiled again, then stumbled with weariness as she left the room. Watching, he ached with tenderness toward her. Between instant motherhood and the house fire, she'd been through a lot in the past twenty-four hours. His sympathetic feelings dissipated when his glance fell on the bulletin board. Felicia's glacial gaze skewered him, reminding him of the capriciousness of women.

Amanda's chortle of delight interrupted his thoughts. She banged her spoon on the tray and stretched her hand toward him, opening and closing chubby fingers. No treachery there.

He cleaned her face gently. "One of the first lessons you have to learn, sweetheart, is that things are seldom as they seem."

WHEN DEVON ENTERED the kitchen after her shower, the room had regained its former order. In her high chair, Amanda played happily with a piece of dry toast, and the aroma of bacon and freshly squeezed orange juice filled the air, making Devon's mouth water.

She welcomed the smells that distracted her from Colin's scent arising from his robe, triggered by the warmth of her body. Standing at the stove with his shirtsleeves rolled to his elbows, snug jeans slung low on his hips and grasping a spatula as easily as if it were hammer or saw, he radiated the easy grace of a man whose identity remained unthreatened by so-called female tasks. She attributed her admiration to the fact that Sara Davis and her television audience would love him.

"Hungry?" His disarming grin made her breath catch.

She slipped into a chair at the newly scrubbed table. "Always, and especially if someone else is cooking."

"Tsk-tsk." He slid two puffy, golden slices of French toast onto her plate and handed her the syrup jug. "Is that any way for the famous Amanda Donovan to talk?"

Her conscience winced. "Amanda Donovan is a myth. I found that out last night."

"And you've decided to confess your true identity to the world?" He filled his plate and sat across from her.

She lowered her eyes and dug into her breakfast. "I can't."

"Why not? A few well-chosen words would clear up the whole mess. For a writer, words should be easy."

She looked up to find him staring at her with granite eyes. "It's not that simple."

"Convince me." He bit into a piece of toast and chewed slowly without diverting his forceful gaze.

She fidgeted beneath his scrutiny. "Amanda Donovan is an icon, a role model to millions of readers. Her advice gives them a sense of confidence, security. Taking that away is like telling a little kid there's no Santa Claus."

His eyes narrowed, telling her he wasn't persuaded. "They're adults. They'll cope."

She shook her head. "If they find I've lied about parts of what I've told them, *everything* I've ever written becomes suspect, and Gramma's advice is too valuable for them to discount any of it."

"How noble," he said in a harsh tone. "And I suppose the quarter-million-dollar payoff for the interview has nothing to do with it?"

She studied the firm set of his square jaw and the glint in his eyes and tried in vain to discern the reason for his cold censure. "I have to make a living. Writing the column is all I know."

"After a look at this kitchen earlier, I won't argue with you on that point."

Amanda shrieked with laughter and pounded her tray with chubby fists.

Devon had to swallow hard to force a bite of French toast past the knot of anxiety in her throat.

His disapproval was palpable, a good indication he'd decided not to help her with the interview.

"Leona's on her way here with the contract," she said. "I'll tell her you've refused."

"But I haven't." He laid his fork on his plate and folded his arms across his powerful chest.

"I don't understand," she said.

"Neither do I."

"But why—"

"Evidently you've done a good job of bamboozling my father. He thinks you walk on water."

Mike. Between the baby and the house fire, she'd almost forgotten. "How is he?"

His posture softened at her question, and worry creased his forehead. "I can't get a straight answer from him or Dr. Packard. It's as if his prognosis is so bad neither one of them wants to say it out loud."

"I'm sorry, because I'm very fond of Mike. Even if you don't do the interview, I'd like for him to move in with me for a while. I'll be happy to take care of him."

He tossed his napkin on the table and stood, raking long fingers through his thick hair. "I told you, I'm *agreeing* to the interview—but only for Dad's sake."

"Because of the bills?" she asked.

"No." He propped his hips against the counter, gripped the edge and crossed his work boots in front of him. "I'd take out a loan if I had to. I'm doing this interview to keep him alive."

She pulled the gaping terry robe closed at her neck and fixed him with a puzzled stare. "You're making absolutely no sense. How can the interview save him?''

''Because he became so agitated when I told him I *wasn't* going to help you, he might have died right then and there.''

Her spirits plummeted, not only with worry for Mike but from the knowledge Colin was helping her only through coercion. But why did that fact hurt so? She'd met him only yesterday, and the man meant nothing to her.

Even as she tried to convince herself of her disinterest, the sight of him, enveloped in worry for his dad, made her long to wrap her arms around his broad shoulders and console him. She gave herself a mental shake. He wouldn't thank her for her comfort.

''So what now?'' she asked.

Amanda gurgled and pitched the battered piece of toast across the kitchen.

Colin turned from observing the baby and grinned at Devon. ''Now, Ms. Amanda Donovan, it's time for your baby's bath,'' he challenged.

The same panicked expression she'd worn when he discovered her amid disaster in the kitchen returned, and again he struggled to stifle his sympathy for her.

''Maybe *you* should bathe her,'' she suggested in a breathless voice.

''You need the practice. What if Sara Davis asks to film you bathing Amanda?''

''Good Lord, do you think she will?'' The color drained from her face.

He shrugged. "You're the celebrity, so you know more about these things than I do."

"But the only living thing I've ever bathed besides myself is a dog I once had, and then I used a hose in the backyard." She threw her hands outward in a gesture of despair that opened the neckline of the robe to reveal the creamy skin of her throat and the swell of her breasts.

The painful irony of the situation taunted him. The family kitchen, a warm and intelligent woman and a charming child—all the things he'd longed for when he'd married Felicia. But they were an illusion. Amanda wasn't his, and Devon was as career-minded and selfish as Felicia had been. Even the homey kitchen wasn't his own.

He averted his eyes from the creamy throat of the tousled-haired beauty before him. "I'll gather up what you need."

He combed the house, collecting mild soap, washcloths and towels, and returned to the kitchen to find Devon at the sink, testing the water with her elbow.

"I'm not totally ignorant," she replied to his inquisitive look. "I remember Gramma's instructions on preparing a bath."

"Then this should be a piece of cake." He handed her the towels and soap. "I'll watch."

Her forehead wrinkled as she appraised the child like an attacking general analyzing battlefield terrain. With studied movements, she spread a towel on the counter by the sink, then lifted the squirming baby from her chair, holding her at arm's length to avoid oatmeal paste. Amanda giggled and kicked her feet when Devon laid her on the towel and removed her diaper.

"Motherhood ought to come with a second set of arms," Devon grumbled, struggling to keep the child from rolling off the counter.

"It usually does," he said, unable to keep the bitterness from his voice. "They're attached to the father."

"Instead of a running commentary, how about some help?" She scooped the naked child into her arms and lifted her toward the sink.

"Wait." He submerged a clean dish towel and spread it across the sink bottom. "This will keep her from slipping."

Devon eased the wiggling baby into the water, holding her tightly with both hands, while Amanda laughed and batted the water with her palms.

"How can I bathe her when it takes both hands to keep her steady?" Frustration laced Devon's voice.

He moved behind her, trying to ignore the length of her slender body pressed against his, reached around and slid one of her hands around the baby's back. "Let her rest on your forearm while you hold her beneath her armpit. Now use your free hand to wash her."

He was helping her support the baby, and his position drew him closer against Devon until her silky hair tickled his nose. She smelled of jasmine and sunshine, and through the terry fabric of the robe, the softness of her body stirred responses within him he thought Felicia had killed forever. He longed to bury his face in her hair, sweep her into his embrace—

Water, splashed in his face by Amanda, jolted him from his musings, and he stepped away, leaving Devon on her own.

He picked up a large towel and spread it across his arms. "If you're finished, I'll take her."

She lifted the dripping baby from the sink and turned toward him. The furrow of concentration between her brows, the unsure expression in her hazel eyes, and the set of her mouth with the tip of a delectable tongue visible between rosy lips made him hunger to gather her along with the sopping baby into his arms.

The chime of the doorbell brought him to his senses.

"I'll get it." Devon deposited Amanda into his outstretched arms and headed for the front of the house. "It's probably Leona."

"I'll dress Amanda," he offered, "and see if I can get her to sleep."

As he headed down the hallway, Leona's voice floated through the house. "Good morning, Devon. How are things progressing?"

"Other than the fact that I'm temporarily homeless," Devon said in a wry tone, "and caring for a child who's bitten me, kept me up half the night, peed on me and spat oatmeal at me, things are going great."

Their voices trailed away as they entered the kitchen, and when he returned to the room a few minutes later, Leona and Devon sat at the table with a sheaf of papers spread before them.

"You don't waste any time, do you, Ms. Wiggins?" he remarked.

Leona threw him a dazzling smile. "With filming for the interview less than a month away, we can't afford to squander time. That's what Devon and I were discussing."

He noted the stack of department-store bags and boxes piled at the table's end.

Devon followed his glance. "Leona brought me some clothes."

"And Devon's told me you've agreed to participate in the show." Leona shoved a document toward him. "If you'll just sign where I've checked, that will make it official."

His conscience rebelled at the entire notion of the deceptive interview, no matter how much money it paid, until he recalled his father, lying weak and helpless in the hospital, clutching his chest and pleading with him. "Help the girl out, Colin, for my sake."

With reluctance, Colin took the pen and signed. "What's next?"

As if afraid he'd change his mind, Leona grabbed the paper and shoved it into her attaché case. "First, you need a wedding on the beach."

"Hold on," he said with a growl. "I agreed to an interview, not matrimony."

Devon flushed. "It doesn't have to be a real ceremony, just something for the videotape Sara wants to use on the show."

"Maybe I've missed out on the discussion," he said, "but if the whole point of this charade is to protect Amanda Donovan's true identity, how are you going to do that *and* have a video filled with wedding guests?''

"What do you mean?'' Devon asked.

"The guests will know the wedding's a fake when it airs on national television.''

Leona dismissed him with a breezy wave. "Devon's creative. I'm sure she'll think of something. As for me, I have to get this contract back to New York.''

DEVON SLIPPED the pale yellow sundress over her head, slid her feet into the sandals Leona had brought and tried to erase Colin's disapproving expression from her mind. For a few moments while they bathed the baby, she'd felt not only physically close to him, but emotionally attuned, as if some invisible conduit of feelings bound them together. Leona's arrival with the contract had severed that connection and brought Colin's censure to the forefront again.

"Why should I care what the man thinks?'' she asked Amanda as she strapped her into the carrier. "Nobody's holding a gun to his head, and he'll be well compensated for his trouble.''

But when Colin met her in the driveway and climbed behind the wheel of his truck, her pulse quickened at the sight of him. She kept her tone businesslike, not wanting him to know he affected her. She'd already proved her incompetence as a parent. Life with Aunt Bessie had left her equally unprepared for a relationship with any man, even one as appealing as Colin O'Reilly.

They drove the few blocks to her house with only Amanda's gurgle of laughter to break the silence. When Colin pulled to the curb behind a truck and a large van marked Restoration Services, her house appeared undamaged, except for smears of oily residue above the windows.

"Once I get my purse and car keys, Amanda and I won't trouble you any longer," she said.

"No trouble." His flat tone contradicted his words. "We'll take over Leona's room since she's checking out today."

He jumped from the truck. "Look, we've already been through this. My dad wants you to stay with me."

She clambered from the truck and confronted him. "But you don't?"

He wouldn't meet her eyes. Tucking his hands into the back pockets of his jeans, he turned to survey the house. "Let's call it a fair exchange. I do your interview, and you humor my father by staying at our house until you can move back into yours."

His cool logic annoyed her. As much as she loved Mike, she didn't believe that living several days in the same house with Colin, who obviously didn't want her there, was such a hot idea, but they needed the time together to prepare for the interview. "Fine. Now will you watch the baby while I find my purse?"

He shook his head. "Let me get it. The restorers should have a go at the inside before you see it again."

His thoughtfulness mollified her ruffled feelings. "My purse is upstairs on the dresser in my room."

Colin headed up the walk, and she nodded to a workman who removed a ladder from the van and carried it into the house. In a few minutes, Colin reappeared with her purse.

"I wiped it down to kill the smoke odor," he said.

"Thanks." She checked the side pocket for her keys. "Did you ask the restorers about my clothes?"

He pulled a bandanna from his pocket and wiped soot from the back of his hand. "They're sorting out what needs to be dry-cleaned. The rest I'll load in the truck and bring back to the house. You can use our washer and dryer."

She nodded and mentally tried to organize the overwhelming number of tasks before her. "I'll stop at the grocery for diapers and formula and meet you at your place."

After a curt nod of acknowledgment, he sprinted back into the house. She reached for her wallet to count her cash, then remembered she'd removed the wallet when she contributed to a solicitor for the high school band the previous morning. Not wanting to make the trip upstairs, she'd shoved the wallet into a drawer of the hall table.

She removed Amanda from the truck, carried her up the driveway to her Honda, unlocked the car and strapped the carrier into the back seat.

"This won't take but a minute, kiddo."

She tossed her purse in the front, then dashed up the walk into the house. Gagging at the stench of stale smoke, she shifted lumber someone had stacked in front of the hall table and retrieved her wallet. The voices of workmen drifted up the hallway from the kitchen, and the temptation to inspect the damage almost drew her to the back of the house until she remembered the baby alone in the car.

She sidestepped lumber and debris to reach the front door, then bounded down the steps and across the lawn toward the driveway. Blinking in disbelief, she stopped dead in her tracks.

Her car—with Amanda in it—was gone.

Chapter Six

For those mothers who choose cloth diapers over the environmentally disastrous disposable ones, changing a squirming child without losing diaper pins in the process presents a challenge. A handy solution is a bar of soap on the changing table in which to push the pins until you're ready for them.

Amanda Donovan, *Bringing Up Baby*

At Devon's shout, Colin raced through the cluttered hall, leaping over stuffed animals and baby furniture before barreling out the front door.

The screech of brakes drew his attention to the center of the street, where a speeding car slammed to a halt within inches of Devon's shapely legs.

"What's the matter with you, lady," the driver yelled. "Are you crazy?"

Without a word or acknowledging glance, Devon scurried across the pavement into the neighbor's yard, where the trunk of her Honda rested among the broken branches of an ornamental kumquat tree.

Colin sprinted down the steps and across the lawn and street to reach the Honda just as Devon removed Amanda from the back seat.

"What happened?" he asked.

She jiggled the child stiffly, and Amanda held out her chubby hands to him. "I just left her for a minute to find my wallet—"

The woman was crazier than he'd thought. "You left her *alone* in a car with the engine running?"

"Of course not! I'd just strapped her in the back seat. I didn't start the car." Splotches of brilliant red stained her high cheekbones, and her lips tightened with anger.

He opened the driver's door and inspected the interior. "The emergency brake isn't on, and you left the car in neutral. When you slammed the rear door, you must have started it rolling."

She glared at him over the baby's silky curls. "The car's been sitting in the driveway for two days. Surely if it had been in neutral, it would have rolled before now." Her eyes widened. "And I didn't close the door, so how—"

"Oh, dear." Devon's plump little neighbor stood on her doorstep, surveying the damage. "You're not hurt, are you?"

Devon shifted Amanda upright against her shoulder. "We're fine, Mrs. Kaplan, but I'm sorry about your lawn and tree—"

"Not to worry." The old lady approached and held out her arms for the baby. "Trees and grass can be easily replaced. What matters is that you're safe. And who's this little princess, a niece of yours?"

Mrs. Kaplan lifted Amanda from Devon's arms with the ease of experience and ran her finger along the baby's dimple. Amanda beamed and grabbed at the woman's glasses.

Colin seethed with outrage. Devon's carelessness could have killed the child, her mad dash into the street could have killed her, too, yet the women stood chatting as if nothing of consequence had happened.

"Amanda's visiting for a while." Devon looked up and down the street as if searching for someone. "Mrs. Kaplan, have you noticed any strangers this morning—anyone loitering around my car?"

With a sigh of disgust, Colin turned away. Why couldn't Devon admit responsibility for her actions? She had to realize her carelessness placed the baby at constant risk.

Mrs. Kaplan stopped cooing and making faces at the child long enough to answer. "Strangers? The neighborhood's been full of them—firemen, police and workmen have been all over your place."

"And just a few minutes ago?" Devon asked.

The old woman shrugged. "I was talking to my sister on the telephone. I can't see your house from the kitchen."

"I'll move the car," Colin said.

Devon agreed without protest and handed him the keys. He climbed into the car and transferred it from Mrs. Kaplan's lawn to Devon's driveway. He waited beside the vehicle while she crossed the street with Amanda in her arms.

"Don't start on me," she warned when she came within speaking distance. "I'm *not* a careless dimwit."

Anger and sunlight flashed in her hazel eyes. She could have been killed, and he was suddenly overwhelmed with an awareness of just how much this spunky woman had begun to mean to him. When she straightened her tanned shoulders and glowered at him, he suppressed the urge to kiss the look of disapproval from her mouth.

Instead, he leaned against the fender and rammed his fists into his pockets. "How do you explain what's happening? First, a suspicious fire—"

"I told you," she interrupted with indignation, "I wasn't using the cooktop. I haven't used it in weeks."

The woman was in major denial. "I stopped by your place this morning on the way to the hospital and spoke with the arson investigator. He said the burned pot held some type of latex, possibly the kind bottle nipples are made of."

Her jaw dropped and she stared at him with an incredulous expression. "Why would anyone *cook* nipples?"

"You're Amanda Donovan. You tell me."

She thought for a moment, then her puzzled look cleared. "You're talking about sterilizing."

"Bingo."

"But I didn't. In fact, I didn't even remember it until you jogged my memory."

Her insistence on innocence bothered him. Either she was refusing to take responsibility for her actions, or someone else really *had* started a fire in her house. "What about the runaway car?"

"Look—" she straightened from securing Amanda in her car seat "—because my driveway is on an incline, I always leave the car in Park with the emergency brake on. That action is as automatic to me as breathing."

He leaned toward her, placing his hands along the roof of the car on either side of her head. He breathed deeply of her jasmine scent and struggled to keep a clear head. "Are you trying to tell me someone else released the brake and put the car in neutral while you were in the house?"

"That's exactly what I'm trying to say, but obviously without effect." She slipped beneath his outstretched arms, adjusting the slender strap of her dress that had slipped over one satiny shoulder, and circled the car to the driver's side.

"But why?" He squinted at her in the sunlight. Not a trace of guilt marked her pretty face, unless the apricot glow of her cheeks was an indication of remorse and not the sun's heat. "It doesn't make sense."

"Which is exactly why all these accidents scare the bejeebies out of me." She climbed into the car, started the engine and backed into the street without a goodbye.

He watched the car disappear around the corner. Maybe she was telling the truth, or maybe the truth was that she'd forgotten to remove the pot from the stove and to set the emergency brake. Devon appeared too intelligent, too competent to cause such accidents, but stress could make people forgetful, and instant motherhood had to be stressful.

She'd either been unbelievably careless or someone was out to harm her and the child. Either way, they'd both need looking after, and between circumstances and his father's pleas, it looked like he'd been elected.

With a sigh of resignation, he sauntered back into the house and began removing damaged wood from the cabinets above the stove while he tried unsuccessfully not to think of his responsibilities toward Devon and the baby.

ERNIE POTTS LEANED on the shelf of the pay phone outside the grocery store that the woman and baby had entered and placed a collect call.

"Yeah, Operator," Muriel answered in a nasal whine, "I'll accept the charges."

"Everything's working out great, sugar," Ernie said.

"That's easy for you to say. You're having a Florida vacation, while I'm here alone, bored out of my gourd, with nothing to do but watch soaps. When are you coming home?"

"Soon." He glanced up as the automatic doors shushed open and an elderly man exited. His quarry was still inside.

"And you're bringing the kid?" his wife demanded.

"Yeah. Things are going even better than I'd planned." He told her about the fire and runaway car.

"Jeez, Ern, are you sure you're not putting the baby in danger?"

"Nah, she'll be fine. She's a cute little thing. You're gonna like her, sugar."

Muriel's giggle rang in his ear. "And you're gonna love her trust fund, aren't ya, sweets?"

A wave of loneliness washed over him at the sound of her laughter. "Tell you what. Since we'll be in the money soon anyway, why don't you catch the bus and join me? You'll have a Florida vacation, and I can use your help."

The doors opened behind him, and the woman came out, pushing a cart filled with groceries and Amanda in the baby seat.

"Gotta go, sugar. If you can't reach me when you get in, take a taxi to the motel."

He strolled behind the woman, climbed into his car and watched her load groceries in her trunk. When she pulled out of the parking lot, he eased his car behind her and followed.

WHEN DEVON LIFTED THE LID of the Dutch oven, the succulent aroma of pot roast, carrots and onions permeated the kitchen. Although the idea wasn't original, Gramma Donovan had often stressed that the best way to a man's heart was through his stomach.

"I'm not getting through to his head or his heart," Devon muttered to Amanda, playing contentedly in the playpen Colin had brought over after the workmen had cleaned it. "And I'm going to need his help not only with this interview but to find out who's making these crazy things happen." She replaced the lid and adjusted the heat. "I'll be out in the garage sorting the laundry, but I'll leave the door open so you can see and hear me."

Amanda giggled and kicked her feet.

Devon shook her head as she entered the garage. "I'm losing it, talking to a kid who can't understand a word I say. And now I'm talking to myself. I'll be stark raving mad before this Davis interview's over and I find the kid a home."

Her nose wrinkled in disgust at the piles of smoke-saturated clothes Colin had spread on a vinyl sheet on the garage floor. She had almost finished sorting them when Amanda's chortling evolved into full-blown rage. Devon scooped up a pile of diapers, flung them into the washer, added detergent and started the wash cycle.

By the time she reached Amanda, the child's face glowed with indignation. A diaper check revealed the source of her tantrum. Devon lifted the child and carried her into the guest room.

Her glance fell longingly on the box of disposable diapers she'd purchased at the grocery store, but remembering the upcoming interview, she decided she needed more practice with the cloth diapers and pins Amanda Donovan advocated, in case an on-camera change was requested.

She removed the sopping diaper and skewered the pins into the bar of soap Gramma Donovan had suggested as the best method to keep from losing them. Amanda's mom and dad had evidently followed that advice, judging from the pinpricked bar she'd discovered among Amanda's things.

She slipped the dirty diaper into a plastic bag that served as a temporary diaper pail and wiped the wiggling bottom with a damp cloth. Amanda's wailing ceased, but the child pitched from side to side, making fastening the clean diaper an athletic ordeal.

"Finally." Devon secured the first pin and brushed the hair from her eyes. "Just one more and you're all set, kiddo."

Amanda stared at her, wide-eyed, then screwed her face into a knot and pitched a fresh tantrum. Holding the diaper together with one hand, Devon reached for a pin with the other, but it was pushed too deeply into the soap and she couldn't extract it. The bar slipped from her grasp and slid to the floor a few feet away.

Holding the baby with one hand, she strained to retrieve the soap, but it was beyond her reach.

"Need some help?"

She jerked up her head at the sound of Colin's voice. One elbow propped against the doorjamb, he observed her with raised eyebrows, then strode into the room, scooped up the errant bar and held it out to her.

Flushing with embarrassment, she yanked the pin free and hastily fastened the diaper.

"Supper will be ready soon," she said.

A muscle twitched in his cheek as if he was trying not to laugh. "I'll run by the hospital to see Dad and be right back."

When he left, Devon clasped the child against her shoulder with weary determination and tried to ignore the high-decibel bellowing in her ear while she prepared a bottle. She returned to the rocker in the guest room and nudged the nipple into the baby's gaping mouth. Amanda's uproar ceased abruptly. As she sucked contentedly, her eyelids drooped.

Moving carefully to prevent awakening the child, Devon carried her back into the kitchen and set her down in the playpen, where she could listen for her while she finished the laundry.

Moving like a zombie after her night with little sleep, she stumbled into the garage and lifted the lid of the washer. Amanda's diapers glared bright pink under the fluorescent lights.

"I don't need this," she moaned, tugging the wet, discolored diapers from the washer. At the bottom of the tub lay her best burgundy silk blouse.

She removed the ruined garment, replaced the colorful diapers and dumped bleach and detergent into the machine. She'd just started the wash cycle again, when a strange odor wafted out from the kitchen. Her pot roast was burning.

With a strangled cry, she raced back to the kitchen and slid the pot off the burner. When she lifted the lid, she viewed with dismay the roast and vegetables already embedded in a tarry black crust on the bottom.

Tears of frustration filled her eyes. So much for impressing Colin with her cooking. After one look at her ruined dinner, he'd consider her a world-class dummy—even if she didn't confess to the rose-colored laundry.

Amanda's babbling noises drew her attention to the playpen, where the baby raised herself on her knees and hands, twisting her bare bottom in the air. Her diaper lay in a corner, where she'd wiggled out of it. Devon hadn't fastened the sides tightly enough.

Defeated, she dropped into a chair, folded her arms on the kitchen table and rested her head on them. Everything she'd touched lately had turned to disaster. Maybe she was losing it. Maybe she really had started the fire and forgotten to set the parking brake. She almost hoped so. She was too tired to handle the idea that someone was out to get her.

WHEN HE RETURNED from the hospital, Colin found Devon asleep at the table and Amanda playing bare-bottomed in her playpen. He quietly lifted the child, carried her to her crib and, after securing her diaper, left her there to sleep.

The kitchen reeked with the smell of scorched food. When he checked the burned contents of the pot, the efforts Devon had made with the meal touched him. Felicia had always been too busy to cook and had insisted on eating out every night.

He tiptoed back to the family room and ordered a pizza on the extension phone. When he returned to the kitchen, Devon had awakened and was surveying her surroundings with the expression of a battle-fatigue victim.

"I burned dinner." Her bottom lip quivered, but she squared her shoulders and looked him in the eye. "And that's not the half of it."

He reached into a cupboard for wineglasses and a corkscrew and withdrew a bottle of zinfandel from the refrigerator and tucked it under his arm. "I wouldn't wish what you've gone through the past two days on my worst enemy. Come into the family room and have a drink."

"But what about dinner?"

"I've ordered pizza."

Her attention flew to the playpen. "Amanda?"

He clasped her elbow and guided her down the hall. "She's asleep in her crib."

Devon collapsed onto the sofa, and Colin sat beside her. With a few twists, he uncorked the zinfandel, filled the glasses and handed her one.

"How's Mike?" she asked.

Her concern touched him. "No change. Doc Packard says he can come home soon."

"I meant what I said about his staying at my house."

He reached out and traced a fingertip from the corner of her eye across her cheek, noting how, even though exhaustion etched her face, she'd agreed to take on another burden. In her unselfishness, she was nothing like Felicia. In fact, Devon Clarke was unlike any other woman he'd ever met.

"With Amanda," he said, "and all the work that needs to be done to your house before the interview, taking care of Dad would be too much."

"Looking after someone you care about is never too much," she insisted. "You just do it."

The late-afternoon sun bathed her face in diffused light and created a golden aura around her short-cropped curls as she smiled up at him with shining eyes and lips moist with wine. Without stopping to think, he lowered his head and covered her lips with his.

For an instant, she returned the pressure, and he slipped his arms around her shoulders, pulling her closer, deepening the kiss. Her soft curves molded against him, and desire hammered through every nerve ending of his body. He slid his hands down the smoothness of her arms, savoring the velvety texture of her skin beneath his fingertips.

The firm pressure of her hands against his chest pushed him away, and she stared at him with bewilderment. "What are you doing?"

He reined in his galloping senses and grinned. "Practicing."

She picked up her glass and sipped her wine, then smoothed her crumpled skirt. "I'm no expert in these matters, but I'd say you're quite competent. Why do you need practice?"

"Have you forgotten already?"

"Forgotten what?"

"The Sara Davis interview. We're supposed to be man and wife, remember?"

She flushed. "But that's all make-believe."

"All the more reason we need the practice." The taste of her, her subtle beauty combined with her vulnerability and her compassion toward his father had provoked a driving hunger in him. He reached for her again, but the chime of the doorbell interrupted.

"The pizza's here," she said with a bright smile and a hint of breathlessness.

With regret, he rose to answer the door.

"HOW CAN YOU PULL this wedding off without jeopardizing your identity?" Colin asked as he backed the pickup down the drive and headed toward the shopping mall.

Devon studied him over Amanda's velvety curls. His attitude had changed two nights ago when she'd burned the pot roast. He'd become less critical, and although he had spent most of his time either working at her house or visiting the hospital, when he returned home, he'd continued to help with Amanda with such an easy grace, natural calm and obvious delight, he'd eased her anxieties about parenting. But he hadn't attempted to kiss her again, and she couldn't decide if she was disappointed or relieved.

During that time, in between caring for the baby, Devon had managed to launder the smoke from her wardrobe and household linens and plan a seaside wedding.

"I contacted a Tampa travel agency," she explained, "one that books tours for foreign tourists who stay in hotels on the beach. The agency's arranged for a busload of foreign visitors to attend our wedding at sunset and enjoy the local color, so to speak."

"You told the agency who you are?"

She retrieved the toy Amanda had tossed and handed it back to her. "Of course not. I just explained we were new to the area, didn't know many people and didn't want to celebrate our marriage alone. With a free buffet and champagne after the ceremony, the agency can provide their clients with an evening's entertainment for the cost of a charter bus."

"Clever girl." He threw her an ambiguous smile. "The tourists will have left the good old U.S. of A. when the Davis special airs, so Amanda Donovan's secret identity is safe."

She nodded. "And I've hired a videographer with a reputation for discretion."

This time, the warmth of his smile was genuine. "With Dad on the mend and your house ready for occupancy tomorrow, it looks like things are under control."

"Don't tempt fate," she warned, trying to ignore the traitorous race of her pulse at his engaging smile.

"Me?" he said with a laugh. "There's not a superstitious bone in my body."

She pulled her rebellious thoughts from how enticingly those bones were structured. "Do you have your list?"

He patted his shirt pocket. "Gray tuxedo, pleated shirt—but does the cummerbund have to be *pink?*"

"Sorry. That's the way I described it in my column, so Sara will be expecting it." She stared out the window at the passing landscape, and the glass reflected her worried frown. "Not everything is under control."

He turned into the mall parking lot and headed toward an empty space near the entrance. "What do you mean?"

"We still don't know who started the fire at my house or why. Or who caused my car to roll across the street."

He parked the truck and turned toward her. Amanda dozed peacefully between them, and the only sound above the idling motor was the gentle whoosh from the air-conditioning vents. The recirculated air teased her with the musky scent of his after-shave.

"If it wasn't you," he said in a dubious tone, "then maybe they were isolated incidents, a random arsonist, a faulty parking brake."

She shook her head. "Both events occurred after Amanda arrived. What if someone's trying to harm her?"

"What would anyone stand to gain by harming a sweet little kid?" His stare intensified, and she looked away.

How could she admit that, according to the provisions of the documents Farnsworth had left her, if anything happened to Amanda, Devon would become the sole recipient of her ample trust fund? Colin already thought she'd caused the accidents. If he learned about the money, he might put two and two together and come up with five, concluding she'd tried to harm the child for financial gain.

Why should you care what he thinks? an inner voice taunted. *The man will be out of your life for good when the interview is over.* The thought provided no satisfaction.

She adjusted her sunglasses, tied a white silk scarf low on her brow and topped it with a wide-brimmed straw hat to hide her appearance while she shopped for a bridal dress. She'd already withdrawn cash from the bank so identification would be unnecessary when she paid for her purchases.

While she unfastened Amanda from her carrier, Colin removed the umbrella stroller from the back of the truck and snapped it open. She lowered the child into the stroller and stood to find him contemplating her disguise.

"I feel like I'm shopping with Mata Hari," he said. "Maybe you should put a mustache and fake nose on the kid, just to be safe."

"Very funny." She gazed at him with alarm. Colin's good looks, his unforgettable physique and face, made him stand out in a crowd. "Babies tend to look alike, but people will remember you."

He opened his mouth as if to protest, then returned to the cab of the truck, where he removed his sunglasses from the visor and put them on. "Okay?"

She shook her head. "Not enough of a change."

"You should have thought of this before we left the house. I don't know what I can do now...."

His glance fell on his toolbox in the truck bed. He pulled out a can of hand-cleaning gel, scooped out a dollop and rubbed it into his thick hair. With a pocket comb, he raked the hair off his forehead and plastered it to his head. His hair, previously the color of rich coffee, gleamed almost black.

Devon giggled and wrinkled her nose at the heavy odor of pine. "The style's a little outdated, but I doubt your own father would recognize you."

"Dear old Dad," he said with a mocking grin. "He's the one who got me into this."

She placed her hand on his arm. "I can't thank you enough. I don't know what I'd have done without your help."

His warm flesh beneath her fingertips sent a tingle up her arm, and she withdrew her hand as if she'd scorched it.

"It's Dad you should thank." His words were brusque, but his smile was friendly as he pushed the stroller toward the mall entrance.

They parted company on the first level. Colin took the escalator to Travino's on the second floor, and Devon and Amanda continued down the concourse to the mall's largest department store.

"May I help you?" The salesclerk who met her just inside the bridal department didn't look a day over fifteen.

"I need a dress for an outdoor wedding." Devon's heart sank at the number of crowded racks before her. When she'd fabricated her wedding column, she'd kept the description of the bridal gown simple, but even so, finding a match would take work. "Something tea-length with a full skirt and off-the-shoulder neckline, suitable for a wedding on the beach."

The clerk eyed Amanda, who was reaching for a bouffant skirt that protruded into the aisle. "This your first wedding?"

Devon pried the baby's chubby fingers from a swatch of *peau de soie* and moved the stroller beyond the reach of the dresses. "What?"

The clerk nodded toward Amanda. "I was just wondering if you wanted white or a pale color."

"Of course I want white. This is my niece. I'm baby-sitting today." The lie rolled off her lips with such ease, her conscience tweaked her.

"I have a couple of dresses that might work." The clerk moved to the back of the store and began sorting through one of the crowded racks.

Devon rolled Amanda toward a display counter and studied the headpieces exhibited among blue garters and prayer-book covers.

"I've found just the dress," the clerk called to her after a few minutes.

Devon turned as the clerk approached with a stunning gown of imported cotton trimmed with an off-the-shoulder collar of Battenberg lace.

"It's beautiful. What do you think, Amanda?" She looked behind her.

The stroller and Amanda had disappeared.

Chapter Seven

When your baby begins to crawl, safety must be your most important priority. A house that is perfectly safe for adults presents a multitude of hazards for a curious child.

Amanda Donovan, *Bringing Up Baby*

Devon's throat closed in panic. Someone had taken Amanda.

"What's wrong?" the clerk asked.

"The baby—help me find her," Devon screamed over her shoulder as she raced down the aisle, batting aside tulle and taffeta to search for the missing child in the deserted bridal section. Her pulse thundered in her ears, and she forced herself to keep moving, while her legs, petrified by fear, felt like wood.

"I'll notify security," the clerk called to her.

Devon hurtled through each department on the first floor, striving to catch a glimpse of anyone pushing a stroller, cornering shoppers to ask if they'd seen anyone with a baby, but no one had noticed a stroller or a child.

When she returned to the bridal section, a mall security guard had arrived.

"Are you the child's mother?" he asked.

"No." Her mind reeled, and in her panic she couldn't remember the lie she'd told the clerk about Amanda. "I'm her guardian."

Attracted by Devon's frantic search and the guard's presence, a small crowd had gathered in the bridal section.

"I'll need a description," the man said.

She took a deep breath and clasped her hands together to stop their shaking. "A baby girl, six months old, blond hair, brown eyes. She's wearing a navy blue dress with a sunflower appliqué and a navy hat with a sunflower on the brim. Her stroller is the collapsible kind with umbrella handles."

"We have a possible kidnapping on the first level. Be on the lookout..." The security guard spoke into a small radio attached to his shoulder and repeated the description.

The clerk dragged a chair from the fitting room and grasped Devon's arm. "I think you'd better sit down."

Devon sank onto the chair but couldn't stop trembling. Poor little kid. Who would do this and why? A number of sinister possibilities flooded her mind, and she shoved them away. They were too horrible to think about.

"Did you see anyone else around before the baby disappeared?" the security guard asked.

She pictured the deserted bridal department and shook her head.

"What's going on here?"

She didn't recognize the slick-haired stranger until he removed his sunglasses and knelt beside her. When Colin circled her shoulders with his arm, his consoling warmth eased her tremors, and she leaned into the solid comfort of his embrace.

"Where's Amanda?" he asked.

"I don't know." She bit her lip to keep from crying.

"You the father?" the guard asked him.

"No, I'm a friend of Ms. Clarke's. Where's the baby?"

"That's what we're trying to find out," the man said. "The police are on their way."

Colin wiped a tear from Devon's cheek, then took her hands in his. "Tell me what happened."

She sagged against him. "I was looking at headpieces in that display. One minute Amanda was in her stroller beside me, the next minute she was gone."

She lifted her head as a policeman shouldered his way through the crowd. After conferring with the mall security guard, he approached Devon and Colin. "Do you know anyone who might want to take the child?"

Devon shook her head.

The police officer pulled out a notebook. "You're the guardian?"

"That's right." She glared at him. "Shouldn't you be looking for her instead of questioning me?"

"Just stay calm, ma'am," the cop said in a soothing tone. "Mall security and several members of our force are searching for her now. The child's not involved in a custody battle, is she?''

"I have full legal custody—her parents are dead."

The policeman shrugged. "I had to ask. Often when children are abducted, the noncustodial parent is the culprit."

Noncustodial. She remembered Farnsworth's insistence that Amanda be kept from her father's half brother, Ernest Potts, whom he'd described as unprincipled. Was the man unscrupulous enough to kidnap his niece?

Where was Amanda now, and what was she doing? Was she crying, longing for a familiar face? Devon recalled how the baby often giggled with delight at the sight of her, and she choked back a sob.

A high-pitched, nasal voice interrupted her thoughts. "I have to talk to the cops. Somebody's left a kid all alone in the ladies' lounge."

A middle-aged woman with frizzy blond hair and a cheekful of chewing gum forced her way through the crowd.

"Where?" Colin asked.

The frowsy blonde propped one hand on an ample hip, lifted the other, tipped with blood red nails, and pointed toward an alcove behind the small-appliance department. The cop took off at a run with Colin close behind. They reappeared a few seconds later with Colin carrying a solemn-faced Amanda while the cop pulled the stroller behind him.

"Amanda!" Devon stretched out her arms, and tears of relief flooded her eyes as she reached for the child. Amanda's face lit up with delight and recognition.

"She's fine. Happy as a pig in mud and doesn't even need a diaper change." Colin handed Amanda to her and drew them both into his arms.

"You oughta know better, lady," the blonde taunted, "leaving the kid alone like that."

Devon felt Colin's muscles go rigid.

"She didn't," the clerk said. "The baby was with her when she came in. I saw them."

The blonde shrugged and faded away into the crowd.

Colin relaxed, hugged Devon to him, then extended his hand to the policeman. "Thanks."

"No problem." The cop pushed the stroller toward Colin. "I guess that settles it, but I'll need your names and addresses for my report."

When the police and security people left, the crowd dispersed.

"I didn't leave her—" Devon began, fearful of the return of his censure.

"It's okay," Colin broke in. "We'll talk about it later. Are you finished here?"

She shook her head. "I barely had a chance to look around before Amanda disappeared. Maybe I'd better take her home and get a sitter before I try shopping again."

Colin reached for Amanda and settled her easily into the crook of his arm. "I'll look after the kid. No need for you to waste a shopping trip."

She contemplated calling off the outing, but decided concentrating on wedding preparations might calm her shattered nerves. "Are you sure you don't mind?"

"I'm being well compensated." He had slipped his sunglasses on, and she couldn't read his expression or the meaning of his ambiguous reply.

Amanda's disappearance had left her badly shaken, and she turned her attention with difficulty to the dress the clerk had selected. Somehow her career and the deception involved in protecting it seemed unimportant in light of this latest near disaster. The sooner she could place the child in a safe home, the better.

When she carried the filmy dress into the fitting room and slipped it on, the reflection in the mirror shocked her. Except for her scarf and sun hat, she looked like a real bride. As she studied her image in the three-way mirror and considered what might have been, she heaved a frustrated sigh.

A make-believe wedding was all she'd ever have, all she'd ever allow. If growing up with Aunt Bessie had taught her little about parenting, it had instructed her even less about the bond between a man and a woman. Although she'd enjoyed dating in high school, she'd never allowed herself to get serious over anyone. Often she'd read that children of divorced parents were more likely to experience divorce themselves. What chance would she have at marital success when she'd never observed any kind of marriage firsthand, not even a rocky one?

In matters of the heart, her grandmother's journals offered little help. Romantically disadvantaged, that's what she was, and a real wedding was definitely not in her future. If she'd had doubts before about her competence in the field of love, her constant confrontations with Colin had proved her ineptness at relating to a man.

She thrust away memories of his kiss and the rightness of his embrace as she smoothed the flattering lines of the dress across her hips and twirled the flared skirt. Might as well enjoy the charade, because playacting was as good as it would get. The only thing Bessie had taught her well was how to succeed as an old maid. Once the interview was finished and Amanda adopted, Colin would leave and her simple life could return to normal.

Normal. Lonely and empty.

She turned a deaf ear to her heart's objections and nodded approval when the clerk suggested white espadrilles with satin laces, perfect for walking through the sand, and a wreath of white silk daisies with satin streamers for her hair.

"Is that the groom?" The teenage clerk gestured toward Colin as Devon paid for her purchases.

When Devon nodded, the clerk sighed. "Lucky girl."

Devon forced a smile in reply. She'd been lucky all right these past few days—and all her luck had been bad.

"Ready to go?" Colin asked. He'd strapped a sleepy Amanda back into her stroller, and when the clerk handed over the packages, he tucked them under his arms and followed Devon, who pushed the stroller out of the store into the mall.

Uneasy, Devon scrutinized each shopper who came close to Amanda, wondering if the person who had whisked her away had followed them. Even Colin's reassuring presence didn't calm her suspicions.

He seemed to read her thoughts. "You're tired and jumpy, and probably hungry, too. I know just what you need."

Fifteen minutes later, under the shade of an umbrella at a waterfront café, she slid into a seat at a table where the warm, salt-laden breeze and water lapping softly against pier pilings siphoned off her tension. Amanda, fed and diapered by Colin, slept in her carrier in the adjoining chair.

When the waitress appeared, Devon allowed Colin to order for her and enjoyed the unaccustomed pleasure of having someone else take charge.

After the waitress had served them tall glasses of iced tea with lime wedges, Colin reached across the table and placed his hand over hers. "Want to talk about it?"

"About what?" Jolted by the surge of emotion created by his touch, she pulled her hand away.

"What happened at the mall. I'm a good listener," he added with a modest grin.

He pushed his chair back from the table and sat with one booted ankle propped on his knee while he stared across the bay toward the barrier islands, shimmering green against the horizon. He'd hooked his sunglasses in his shirt pocket, and his unprotected eyes reflected the brilliant emerald of the water like polished pewter. Strength and a bolstering calm emanated from him, and for the first time since Amanda had disappeared in the store, Devon's nerves quieted.

"What do you think it all means?" she asked.

He rubbed the strong line of his jaw thoughtfully. "Whatever it is, it's tied up with the baby."

"But none of this makes sense," she insisted. "Whoever set the fire apparently intended more smoke than heat. And the same person probably caused my car to take off with Amanda in it."

"And today in the store?"

Her eyes widened at the implication. "If the same person is involved, I'm being followed."

"But why? If someone wants to take the baby, he— or she—could have grabbed Amanda that day you left her in the car. Why wait to grab her in a crowded mall?"

"Maybe somebody just wants to scare me." She gave a nervous laugh. "If that's the case, they're doing a heck of a job."

"Which raises another question. Why is this person intimidating you?"

She shrugged. "If they're hoping I'll give up the baby, I'm way ahead of them. I plan to put Amanda up for adoption as soon as possible."

Disgust flickered across his face. "You'll wait until after your important interview, of course."

She longed to explain that adoption was the best thing for the child, providing her with two parents and maybe brothers and sisters, but most of all, with someone competent to care for her. Yet if she confessed how inadequate she felt to raise a baby, she feared he'd be more repulsed than ever.

His disgust gave way to thoughtfulness. "You said her parents are dead. Are there any relatives who'd want her enough to terrorize you into giving her up?"

She nodded. "Ernest Potts, Amanda's father's half brother. Potts, according to the attorney, is dishonest, and Amanda's father insisted the child be kept away from him."

His gaze strayed to the child, asleep in the shade, and his features softened. "I can understand why he'd want her. She's such a sweetheart."

"If it was Potts, why didn't he take her today when he had the chance? Why leave her in the ladies' lounge?"

His gaze returned to her and his expression hardened once more. "Maybe he didn't have enough time before security was alerted. He'd never have made it out of the mall with her."

Her heart wrenched with an amazing pain at the thought of losing little Amanda. She'd have to start adoption proceedings soon, or giving her up would be too difficult.

For the first time, she entertained the idea of raising the child herself. Images of Amanda's first steps, her first day at school, her first bike, flitted through her mind. She repressed the thoughts quickly. Such a situation would be a repeat of her solitary life with Aunt Bessie, and the helpless orphan deserved more.

Colin folded his arms on the table and leaned toward her. "The restoration supervisor says you can move back in tomorrow. I'll install a home security system, if you like."

She studied the corded muscles of his arms beneath the rolled sleeves of his denim shirt, the resolute set of his square jaw, the steely look in his gray eyes. With such a man, any woman would feel safe, protected. But in her rent-a-husband world, she'd have to settle for security of the electronic kind.

"Thanks," she said. "Amanda and I will be much safer with a central-station alarm."

The sun's angle had shifted while they talked, and Colin adjusted the umbrella to shade Amanda. Again his expression mellowed at the sight of the child.

"You love kids, don't you?" she observed.

"Not so loud. You'll ruin my macho image." He spoke with a light tone, but she could see the pain in his eyes.

Felicia must have hurt him badly.

"I forgot about your wife." She pressed her palm to her forehead as the new complication struck her. "What if she makes trouble after she sees the interview?"

"*Ex*-wife," he countered with a bitter edge. "Don't worry. Felicia will be too concerned about any possible stain on her own career to raise questions about yours."

"What does she do?"

"She's a real-estate broker, and a very successful one, I might add." His words rang like the sharp, cold clink of the ice he swirled in his glass. "She left me so she could spend more time selling houses to wealthy clients."

"I'm sorry."

"Don't be. It was for the best."

"Then why are you so angry?" Her question popped out like a reflex. "Forgive me. That's none of my business."

He hesitated, as if deciding whether to answer. "Dad's encouraged me to talk about it, to get it off my chest. He says I hold things in and let them fester."

He paused while the waitress placed plates of chicken salad before them.

"Felicia's very pretty," she said, remembering the snapshot on the kitchen bulletin board and the ice blue eyes.

"Yes, she is," he replied with a swiftness that sent a twinge of jealousy through her. "We met at an exhibition of homes I'd designed for a Tallahassee builder. Felicia's agency was handling sales."

"So you had a lot in common."

"I thought we did. I was wrong." He shoved his plate away as if he'd lost his appetite. "She swore she was interested in a home and family, but she changed her tune after our marriage. Glitz and glamour excited her more than family, and children would only clutter her decorated interiors and soil her designer clothes."

No wonder he looked at Amanda with longing eyes. He yearned for the kind of family life his father and mother had enjoyed, but he'd chosen the wrong woman to help him fulfill his dream. And no wonder he seemed so displeased with Devon. Between her newspaper career and her refusal to keep Amanda, she was too much like Felicia.

"You're young," she said with a sinking heart, realizing how much she wished she could be the kind of woman he sought. "There must be thousands of women who want a home and family and would jump at the chance to marry you."

"It's always been just my luck to fall in love with the wrong woman."

She paused as she reached for her glass. At first she thought he'd been referring to Felicia, but his tortured look as he scrutinized her across the table made her wonder what he was really thinking behind the hurt in his eyes. The possibility that Colin might care for her created a warm rush of pleasure, succeeded by panic.

How did she get herself into such a mess? She was up to her eyeballs in a deception that would be aired on national television, she'd become the totally inept guardian of a baby, and now she was falling in love, a state about which she knew even less than she did about raising children.

She dabbed her lips with her napkin and threw Colin a shaky smile. She'd been cursed, as the Chinese proverb said, by living in interesting times.

COLIN HALTED ON the threshold of the family room, looking for Devon. Whoever had started the fire in her house, tampered with her car and then taken Amanda had put her and the baby through a harrowing ordeal, but the stress hadn't dampened Devon's pluck or her energy. Without a word of complaint, she'd moved back into her restored house as if nothing had happened. Several times he'd wanted to apologize for doubting her about the fire and unattended car, but through the long, bitter years with Felicia, he had become too accustomed to swallowing his responses, and his apology remained unspoken.

He spotted Devon as she scooted on her stomach from behind the sofa and crawled into a corner beneath a table. The sway of her small, rounded bottom activated a searing heat deep inside him. But his response was more than physical. He craved to shield her from all unpleasantness, to spend as much time as he could with this appealing woman who never failed to surprise him, like now, crawling beneath the furniture like some domestic commando.

"Did you lose something?" he asked.

Startled by his voice, she jumped up and banged her head against the table. Holding her brow with one hand, she scuttled backward and stood, straightening her shirttail over crisp white shorts.

"I'm getting ready to babyproof," she said.

He laughed. "As an architect, I know something about making a house safe for children, but I can't see how sliding around on your stomach helps."

Her cheeks flushed an alluring pink. "Gramma Donovan—"

"I might have known." He rolled his eyes and grinned. "What does the maven of motherhood have to say on the subject?"

"Just good common sense," she answered in a miffed tone. "She recommends getting on the baby's level to check for hazards. It's a whole new perspective down there. You should try it sometime."

Chastised, he yielded to her logic. "Just let me know what you want done beyond the usual socket protectors and cabinet locks, and I'll take care of it."

"Thanks." She inspected the front of her clothes. "The restorers did a great job. Not a trace of soot in the entire house."

"I've heard of white-glove inspections, but a full-body sweep is new to me." He wrenched his gaze from her firm breasts, the slender waist that swelled into sensuous hips, her lithe, long legs and bare feet. "Is Amanda asleep?"

"Finally. She's such a curious little thing, afraid if she goes to sleep, she'll miss something." She pointed to the monitor on the coffee table. "Those are great, aren't they? I don't have to keep running upstairs to see if she's awake."

"Are you sure it's working?"

"I heard her babbling to herself before she drifted off to sleep." She retreated with a natural grace into the kitchen and poured coffee into mugs. "Did you get Mike settled at home?"

"He went to bed right after supper. He sends his thanks for your offer to stay here, but says he's more comfortable in his own bed. And he insists he's coming here to work in the morning."

"Work? Didn't the doctor tell him to take it easy?"

She handed him a mug and folded her long legs into the corner of the sofa opposite him. Concern etched her face, and he couldn't help comparing her to Felicia again. His ex-wife would have whined about the delay in remodeling, but the state of Mike's health was Devon's chief concern.

"I spoke with Doc Packard," he said. "He believes light work will be the best thing for Dad—as long as there's no heavy lifting. It will occupy his mind and keep him from worrying about his heart."

"It'll be good to have him here. I've missed him." She smiled with a genuineness that grazed his heart.

"Dad also insists on being best man at the wedding next week." He anticipated the usual annoyance that bubbled up whenever he considered the deception of the wedding and interview, but in its place came a sweet sadness that their relationship was only sham.

"Everything's ready." She ticked the items off on her fingers. "Photographer, caterer, guests, Leona, who'll serve as bridesmaid, and Jake Blalock, my old editor, who'll pose as the minister."

"Then why do you look so uneasy?" He scooted closer and traced the furrow between her brows with his index finger.

She shivered at his question. "Murphy's Law, I guess. The more I consider this entire scheme, the more possibilities for disaster I see."

Unable to stop himself, he reached out and stroked her red-gold curls, glossy as silk beneath his palm. "I warned you of the pitfalls from the first."

"I know." Her breathless voice was barely audible. "I wish I could call the whole thing off."

He reached deep inside himself in an attempt to resurrect his former anger and disdain, but all he found was tenderness. He slid his hand down to the back of her neck and felt her warmth and delicacy against his flesh.

"It's too late now." His words rang with double meaning.

She gazed up at him, hazel eyes wide and clear, lips slightly parted. She could save him from himself by pulling away, but she remained in his grasp, unmoving.

He brushed his lips across hers, and she remained still, as if waiting. When he pulled back and caught the light shining in her eyes, he knew he was doomed. He wrapped his arms around her, drew her close and kissed her the way he'd wanted to ever since he'd first seen her, standing firm in spite of her fear, wearing a coffee-soaked T-shirt and demanding to know who he was.

Devon gasped with pleasure. Nothing in Gramma's journal or her platonic dates had prepared her for such a kiss. With his hand against the small of her back, he drew her to him, and the heat of his powerful body radiated through hers. His lips were firm yet soft, and generated waves of pleasure to her very core.

Her breath mingled with his, and she pressed against him, wanting more, opening her lips to his deepening kiss. Every nerve tingled with awareness of the hard breadth of his chest, the strong line of his thigh snug against her own.

When he lifted his lips from hers and pulled her head into the hollow of his throat, she snuggled deeper into his embrace with a tremor of satisfaction.

"Colin," she breathed with a sigh that was both prayer and benediction.

"Guess we'll fool them pretty good at the wedding ceremony." His voice was husky with emotion as he stroked her hair with his strong, square palm.

Her common sense revived at his words. "You mean this is just practice?"

Before he could answer, a heavy thud sounded over the baby monitor.

Devon pulled away and jumped to her feet. "Good Lord, Amanda's fallen out of bed."

Colin shoved past her, racing toward the stairway. "Not at her age. Someone's in her room. Call the police."

The kidnapper had returned. Her heart leaped into her throat, squeezing off her breath. She stumbled to the phone and punched 911 with shaking fingers.

When the operator answered, Devon forced out her address. "Someone's trying to steal my baby. They're upstairs now. I can hear them."

Footsteps, another thud and a muffled curse reverberated through the monitor.

"Stay on the line, ma'am," the operator's calm voice instructed her. "We have a cruiser in your neighborhood. It's on the way."

Devon's instinct was to hang up and rush to Amanda, but she knew Colin would protect the child. But who would protect Colin? What if the kidnapper was armed and dangerous?

Footsteps thundered down the stairs.

"I have to go—"

"Stay on the line, ma'am. The officers are almost there."

Again the beat of footsteps on the stairs resonated through the house. Wracked with anxiety, fearful Amanda had been snatched away and Colin injured, she fought between obeying the operator and running to help. Swallowing her panic, she stayed by the phone while long minutes dragged past.

"The police are at your front door now," the operator said. "Can you let them in?"

Devon dropped the receiver and raced down the hall toward the front door. Two uniformed officers the size of small buildings stood on the porch.

"Upstairs," she cried. "Someone's stealing my baby!"

The first officer bounded up the stairs toward the bedroom, while the second pulled her aside. "Go tell the 911 operator we're inside, then hang up." As she turned toward the kitchen, he grasped her arm. "Are these the only stairs to the second floor?"

She nodded.

"Then stay in the back of the house, out of the way, until one of us comes for you."

"Colin's up there—" she began.

"We'll take care of him. Just go to the back of the house and stay put. If you're in the way, you could get hurt or obstruct our efforts."

Devon raced to the kitchen, delivered the message to the operator, then hovered over the monitor. Several loud thuds, the noise of scuffling, a muted shout and Amanda's shrill cries reverberated through the speaker. Devon clasped her hands over her mouth to keep from crying out. She'd never forgive herself if anything happened to Colin or the baby.

Chapter Eight

Never underestimate the importance of the family and extended family upon a child. Babies need the security of parents, siblings, grandparents and aunts and uncles as they grow and develop. How a baby relates to family often determines how well the child will fare in later life.

Amanda Donovan, *Bringing Up Baby*

Devon had exhausted every ounce of self-restraint. She barreled up the hall and collided with an officer as he stepped off the stairs with a tearful Amanda in his arms. She retrieved the child and clutched the sobbing baby against her thumping heart.

"We caught him, ma'am," the officer said.

"Thank God." She slumped with relief against the paneled wall.

Footsteps sounded on the stairs above her, and the other officer shoved a man in handcuffs ahead of him.

Colin lifted his shackled wrists. His granite jaw tensed as he glared down at her with fierce eyes. "Tell them who I am. They don't believe me."

She shuddered at his furious gaze. How had the officer confused Colin with the kidnapper? She confronted the policeman beside her. "You have the wrong man. The real kidnapper is getting away."

At her words, the officer darted out the door, while his partner released Colin. "Sorry. We didn't know there was another adult in the house. Stay here while we check outside."

After the second officer followed his partner, she closed the door behind him and leaned against the frame.

Colin rubbed his wrists and confronted her with an ironic grin. "He jumped me from behind when I tried to follow the intruder out the window. Is Amanda okay?"

Amanda's tears had ceased, and she nestled contentedly against Devon's neck. Drowsiness weighted her tiny eyelids and golden lashes brushed her plump cheeks, flushed pink with sleepiness.

Devon nodded. "She seems fine now. Tell me what happened."

The longing expression on his face as he pulled her and the child to him triggered a heat deep within her, and she reveled in the secure feeling of his arms around her. The warmth of human contact had been missing all her life. Aunt Bessie had not been a demonstrative person. A pat on the shoulder and a peck on the cheek on birthdays and Christmas had been the extent of her physical affection. But inexperienced as Devon was in such matters, she recognized the difference between the touch of kin and the puzzling mixture of electricity and calm produced by Colin's embrace. She snuggled deeper into his arms, cradling Amanda between them. She could easily become accustomed to such a haven.

The foolishness of her thoughts struck her like a blast of arctic air, and she pulled away. She was no better equipped for emotional involvement with Colin than she was for performing brain surgery. With a heaviness weighting the center of her heart, she turned back toward the family room and settled in the rocker, careful not to disturb the sleeping baby.

"Do you want me to hold her?" The smooth sound of his deep, rich voice sent her nerve endings humming again.

"I don't want to wake her." Reluctant to give her up, Devon tightened her arms around the child and silently dismissed her personal dilemma. Amanda's safety was foremost. What if she hadn't had a monitor? Where would Amanda be now? The thought terrified her, and she cuddled the child closer to keep her hands from shaking. "Did you see who it was?"

Colin shook his head. "When I reached her room, the door was locked from the inside. I ran downstairs for a crowbar, but by the time I jimmied the door, the intruder was gone—out the window."

She pulled her gaze from the dark anger in his eyes. "How did he get inside?"

"I think I know." Colin disappeared into the hall and returned in a few minutes. "I had the living room windows open to air out the paint fumes. The screen of a window off the front porch has been removed. He probably planned to sneak Amanda out the same way."

"Why didn't we hear him?" she asked. "He was just a few feet away."

"I guess we were busy." The anger in his eyes dissolved, replaced with a glow like molten steel. He looked as if he wanted to kiss her again.

She flushed, remembering the intensity of his kiss. The sound of heavy footsteps in the hall startled her from her recollection.

One of the policemen appeared in the doorway. "We've done a thorough check of the yard, but there's no sign of anyone. We'll interview the neighbors. They might have noticed something. Otherwise, there's not much we can do."

"Thanks for coming so quickly," she said.

The officer replaced his cap and tapped the brim in salute. "Sorry we couldn't be more help, ma'am."

Colin walked him to the door, and when the murmur of their voices ceased, Devon heard the sound of locks and latches turning as Colin secured the door and windows before returning to her.

"What if the kidnapper comes back?" she asked.

"I'll sleep with you tonight."

She forced herself to avoid his eyes. Their warm velvet reflected her own longing, and the implications of his statement made her throat go dry.

"With me?" As she fought against her welling desire, she focused on the baby and assumed a light tone. "I doubt sleeping together is something Sara

Davis expects for her interview, so we don't need the practice.''

He grasped the arms of the rocker and leaned toward her, his lips inches from her, tension crackling in the air. "Do you really think that's what I meant?"

His nearness sucked the breath from her lungs. His woodsy scent tinged the air. She couldn't think, breathe. She inhaled with a desperate gasp, seeking escape.

She rocked backward, forcing him to release the chair, and smiled. ''Of course not. You're suggesting Amanda and I use the guest room at your father's again.''

He scoured her face, pinning her eyes with his own, as if he knew what thoughts lay behind them. When he raked his fingers through his thick hair and sank onto the sofa, she expelled a sigh of relief. He'd retreated—for now.

''Dad will love having you and the baby there,'' he said in a neutral tone. ''Tomorrow, I'll finish installing your alarm system.''

She had her own plans for tomorrow. While Colin worked, she'd contact an attorney. Anonymity was Amanda's only hope for keeping out of the hands of Ernest Potts, if that's who the kidnapper was. Adoption by a couple in another part of the country, far away and unknown to anyone, would keep the child safe.

And visiting the attorney will keep me away from Colin and the desire his nearness creates.

Amanda stirred against her breast and sighed in her sleep, and a sense of loss pierced Devon with savage power. Now she'd really gone and done it. She'd not only fallen in love with the irresistible architect-turned-carpenter, but the child, as well, and both affections were certain to bring her nothing but regrets.

"OUCH, DAMMIT, that hurts!" Ernie winced as Muriel laid the ice pack across his swollen ankle.

"Serves you right, you big goof." She adjusted the pillow beneath his foot, then fluffed the one behind his head. "Jumping out of second-floor windows at your age."

"I didn't jump. I slid down a vine until I was a few feet from the ground and landed wrong."

"You're lucky you didn't land in jail." Muriel paused before the mirror and dabbed a smear of lipstick from the corner of her mouth. "I almost had a heart attack when that police car came speeding down the street past me. Good thing I kept the engine running."

Ernie chuckled and ran a hand over the day-old stubble on his chin. "They were necking like a couple of teenagers. I would've been in and out of there before anybody noticed if it hadn't been for that blasted intercom. Nobody had those when I was a kid."

"You're talking about a *long* time ago, sweets." She kicked off her high-heeled sandals, picked up a magazine and stretched out beside him. "Nobody had computers or car phones then, either."

He folded his arms behind his head and smiled. "Even with this bum ankle, things worked out. I didn't even have to call the cops. The young broad did it for me."

Muriel's forehead wrinkled, crazing her makeup. "I still don't understand why you wanted cops there."

Wincing at the pain in his ankle, he pulled himself into a sitting position. "I wanted them to look like bad parents. I had planned to lock the kid in the room. Make them have to call the cops or a locksmith—anybody who'd keep a record that they'd cut themselves off from the kid."

"Yeah." She nodded, then her eyes clouded. "I still don't get it."

He sighed and patted her lush behind. Lucky for him Muriel had assets to compensate for her simple mind. "That record will be evidence in my case against them."

"Yeah, but now the police think someone tried to take the kid."

"Nobody saw me, so they can't prove nothing, except the kid was locked in her room."

Muriel stopped flipping pages and shoved the magazine toward him. "Look at this ad. I can't wait to have a little girl to dress in cute clothes like these. Maybe I'll even bleach her hair so she'll look like me. People will think she's really mine."

He heard the wistfulness in her voice and remembered how she'd longed for children of her own. Now he was going to set things straight. She'd have her baby, and best of all, he'd have Chad's money.

He lay back and closed his eyes. Everything was working to his advantage. It was just a matter of time.

DEVON STRETCHED, easing her back muscles that had stiffened from sitting, and glanced at the clock. Almost noon. She turned back to her computer and had just typed the ending of next week's column when a light tap sounded at her bedroom door. She swiveled her chair away from her desk to discover Mike, dressed in work clothes and wearing his tool belt, standing in the doorway.

She jumped up and took him by the arm. "You shouldn't have climbed those stairs."

He shrugged. "I'm not even out of breath."

"Sit here." She maneuvered him into a chair beside her desk.

"You mustn't fuss," he said. "Doc says exercise is the best thing for me."

"Just don't push it. I like having you around." As she resumed her seat, worry for the old man, who had filled the place of the father she'd never known, squeezed her heart.

"You're the one who's pushing it, my girl. Out of bed before the crack of dawn. Mysterious telephone calls after breakfast. An early-morning appointment downtown, and now slaving away at your computer." He reached over and patted her hand. "What's going on?"

"It's time to fix lunch." Purposely avoiding his question, she started to rise, but he caught her hand.

"Not so fast. Mrs. Kaplan, your lovely widowed neighbor, is downstairs making sandwiches while she watches Amanda, so you have plenty of time to tell old Mike what's chased the sunshine out of those pretty hazel eyes."

Affection for the old man who could read her like a book rushed over her. She settled for a half-truth. "I'm worried about Amanda."

"Colin will have the alarm system working before the end of the day. And he'll be staying here at night until the kidnapper is caught."

Her eyes widened. "He can't stay here!"

Mike regarded her with a broad grin that creased the leathered skin around his twinkling azure eyes. "Are you afraid people might talk?"

"Of course not." How could she tell him she feared her own desire? The thought of Colin, sleeping on the sofa in the room beneath her, created a warm tingling deep in her abdomen. Then she remembered Mike's illness and, wondering if two half-truths made a whole, uttered another one. "I don't want you left alone. You've been ill and—"

"Don't you fret that very pretty head about me." His voice rang with gentle firmness. "My older daughter, Betsy, is arriving today from Orlando for a couple weeks. I won't be able to draw breath without Betsy checking on me."

"Clearing all this up will take more than a couple weeks," she said with a sigh.

"This? You mean catching the kidnapper?"

His question caught her off guard. She'd been thinking of the interview, her dangerous attraction to his handsome son, and how all the facets of her life tangled together in the major deception she'd concocted for Sara Davis—her work, the baby, Colin—as well as the threats to Amanda.

She shoved her fingers through her hair in frustration and returned to Mike's question. "If the kidnapper is smart, he'll lie low for a while. And if it's Ernest Potts, as I suspect, he might even head back to the Midwest until things cool down here."

Mike covered her hand with his callused one. "By then you'll have your alarm—"

"But that only helps when I'm home. I'm scared to step outside with Amanda for fear someone will snatch her away." She threw him a wry smile. "Even Amanda Donovan can't watch a baby every second."

He studied her with shrewd eyes. "Where did you go this morning?"

She exhaled a deep sigh of resignation, conceding she couldn't keep her morning's mission a secret forever. "I had a meeting with an attorney. He's checking for any legal recourse to stop Farnsworth from revealing Amanda Donovan's true identity."

"And?" Mike's white eyebrows peaked in a questioning gaze.

She fidgeted beneath his stare. "And I asked him, as soon as Farnsworth is taken care of, to start adoption proceedings to place Baby Amanda in a permanent home."

His eyes widened in surprise. "Adoption? You'd really give her up?"

A swift pain burrowed deep into the center of her heart at the thought of losing the child. "What choice do I have? I'm a single woman with no experience, and the baby needs a real home. Her trust fund will guarantee her financial security—"

"Trust fund?"

"It comes with the guardianship." When she mentioned the amount, he whistled.

"That much money would make things a lot easier for you," he said.

"I haven't touched any of it—it wouldn't be right. I opened an account in Amanda's name this morning and deposited the first check."

He stroked his chin thoughtfully. "I know how much we wrestled to keep costs down on this remodeling. Won't you need that trust money to pay the lawyer?"

She shook her head. "That's where the interview proceeds come in. Whatever I earn from Sara Davis will pay to insure Amanda has a good home."

"That's mighty unselfish," he said with an admiring grin.

She flushed at his praise and shook her head. "It's just doing the right thing. But please promise you won't mention any of this to Colin."

"What's Colin got to do with it?" His wise expression suggested he knew more than he professed.

"Every time I mention adoption, he looks at me as if I just crawled out from under a rock." She shuddered, remembering Colin's disdain. "I can't make him understand the child needs a mother and father, brothers and sisters."

Mike gathered both her hands in his work-worn ones and squeezed them gently. "Aren't you going about this backward?"

She feigned ignorance. "What do you mean?"

"Instead of looking for parents for Amanda, you should find yourself a husband. Then *you* can provide the brothers and sisters Amanda needs."

She swallowed the panic his suggestion provoked. "I'm not marriage material, Mike."

He gave her hands another squeeze, then released them, but his clear blue gaze skewered her. "You didn't think you were mother material, either, but look how you've handled Amanda. My own Katie couldn't have done better."

"You really think so?" Satisfaction cascaded through her at his words.

"Absolutely." He rose to his feet. "Now, how about some lunch?"

"You go on. I'll be down as soon as I've transmitted this week's column to the syndicate."

She watched him leave with a spring in his step, unusual for someone who had been so ill only a week before, but she was glad he was mending. Dear old Mike. His compliments boosted her confidence in her parenting skills, but they did nothing to reassure her about the idea of marriage. As daunting as bringing up a baby was, parenting was a picnic compared to the skills necessary for a permanent relationship with a man.

Even a man like Colin?

She thrust the thought away. What she really needed was advice on what to do when Colin's kisses turned her knees to water or when her heart leaped into furious pounding whenever he entered the room. She needed someone to explain how to deal with him when her words displeased him or she couldn't make him understand how she felt. Gramma's journals, aside from suggestions for feeding a man well, provided no help at all in that department.

She relayed her column over the phone line and hurried downstairs for lunch. When she reached the foot of the stairs, Colin came through the front door with a flat of potted flowers tucked under one arm.

She halted on the bottom stair and gripped the newel to stop herself from running to him. The bright Florida sun outlining his muscular physique, the flowering plants beneath his strong, tanned arm and a look in his eyes warm enough to incinerate icebergs resurrected every memory of his touch, of his lips on hers.

She struggled for objectivity. "Your dad says lunch is ready."

"Looks like you've caught me with the goods." He inclined his head toward the plants. "I was hoping to surprise you."

"Those are for me?" Joy surged inside her, but she tamped it down, refusing to place importance on it. He worked for her, after all. Maybe the flowers were part of his job. "Are they for the yard?"

He laid the flat across some nearby sawhorses and dusted his hands. "The fire killed the plants in your kitchen window. I saw these while I was at the home store and thought they'd make a good replacement."

She stepped into the hall and examined the ruffled jade leaves and pale yellow blossoms that suffused the air with a sweet, peppery fragrance. "They're beautiful. What are they?"

He moved behind her, and although he didn't touch her, her nerves danced with an awareness of his closeness. "A new geranium hybrid. They're the color of sunshine, so they reminded me of you."

His voice caressed her, enveloping her in its richness. She'd never longed to kiss anyone as much as she wanted to kiss him at that moment, but she breathed deeply, willing the urge to pass. Of course the flowers reminded him of her. Wasn't every room in her house some shade of delicate yellow? She shouldn't look for meaning where there was none.

But when she turned to face him, her common sense couldn't deny the emotion in his eyes. All her senses clicked on alert. She tried to tug her gaze away, but she couldn't move.

"Mom always had flowers in her kitchen window," he said with a whimsical softness in his voice. "Makes a place feel more like home."

She nodded and swallowed the lump his tenderness had brought to her throat. "They'll be good for the interview."

"I wasn't thinking of the interview." Fire blazed in his gray eyes as he reached behind her, placed a firm hand between her shoulder blades and drew her to him, then dipped his head and covered her lips with his.

She responded with a ferocity that frightened her back to her senses. With both hands planted on the broad expanse of his denim shirt, she pushed away. "This is pointless."

He cocked his head and fixed her with a skeptical grin. "Why?"

She brushed the back of her hand across lips that throbbed from the pressure of his mouth. "Because there's no future in it."

His eyebrows lifted. "Did you enjoy it?"

A flush started at her collar and spread upward across her face. "That's irrelevant."

"Irrelevant? Enjoyment is the whole point."

He reached for her again, and she sidestepped his arms, banging her shin against a sawhorse. The flat of plants tipped, and Colin caught them just before they hit the floor. While he juggled the plants, she scooted down the hall beyond his reach.

"Lunch is ready," she called over her shoulder.

"Devon."

The sound of her name on his lips stopped her. At the far end of the hall, she looked back at him. With a graceful motion, he lifted the flat of plants and strode toward her. The flowers' peppery fragrance, Colin's special scent of maleness and wood shavings, his rich voice echoing in her ears and the overpowering nearness of him set her senses on overload.

She backed away. "What do you want?"

He leaned toward her, planted a fleeting kiss on the tip of her nose, then grinned with the look of a man well pleased with himself.

"I want to teach you how to enjoy life," he said.

Her back stiffened with indignation. "I don't need anyone to teach—"

He stifled her response with another quick kiss, this one on her lips. She should pull away. She could feel Mike and Mrs. Kaplan observing them through the open doorway, but she couldn't move, except to rise on tiptoe to meet the pressure of Colin's lips with her own.

As quickly as he had swooped down on her, he withdrew, and the laughter twinkling in his eyes reminded her of his father.

"Lesson number one will start tonight. Now let's eat."

He proceeded into the family room and left her standing stunned in the hall, struggling for breath and wondering how in a few short days she'd managed to turn her whole life into an adventure that scared her senseless.

Chapter Nine

A reliable baby-sitter is a young mother's most valuable resource. Enlist a grandparent or aunt, a trusted neighbor, or a capable teenager to care for your child while you attend those events and occasions not appropriate for children or simply to give yourself a needed break.

Amanda Donovan, *Bringing Up Baby*

Mike had gone home to welcome Betsy, and Mrs. Kaplan had returned to her house across the street. Devon raised her eyes from the sunny cabbage roses on the chintz slipcover she was stitching to watch Colin on his hands and knees, rolling a pull toy back and forth on the hardwood floor in front of Amanda.

Devon jabbed the needle through the cloth, pricking her finger. The pain reminded her that the scene before her was a sham, make-believe bliss invented solely for the Sara Davis interview. Why had she allowed herself to become so entangled in deception?

To find the baby a good home and keep your own house and job, her heart reminded her, while her head chastised her for attempting more than she could handle. She had created perfect domestic bliss for columnist Amanda Donovan, but how was plain old Devon Clarke going to feel when the television lights went out and Colin and Baby Amanda disappeared from her life forever?

The baby giggled with delight and clapped her hands before lunging for the plaything. Colin's voice blended with the child's delighted laughter in the family room, driving Devon's misgivings away and filling her with a sweet contentment.

Colin lifted his head and stared at her over Amanda's golden curls. "Time for the lessons I promised you."

"You're being presumptuous." She hadn't forgotten their conversation before lunch, and at his reminder, her momentary bubble of well-being shattered around her. "I am perfectly capable of enjoying myself."

He sat back on his heels, folded his muscled forearms across his broad chest and viewed her with a grin that tilted one corner of his mouth. "Convince me."

With the uncomfortable feeling she'd just engaged in a battle she was sure to lose, she squirmed beneath his gaze. "Why should I?"

"So I'll leave you alone. That's what you want, isn't it?" he challenged.

"No!" The intensity of her denial flustered her, and she struggled to cover her embarrassment at revealing how fervently she wanted him to stay. "I just don't want anyone believing I'm a drudge."

"Like I said—"

"I know, convince you." She secured her needle in the cabbage-rose chintz and set it aside with a deliberate motion designed to give her time to think.

He scooped Amanda up from the rug, settled into the chair beside the sofa and bounced the child gently on his knee. "Well?"

Devon scrambled through her memories, searching for examples of her ability to have fun, but since Aunt Bessie's death, her life had revolved solely around her column and restoring the Victorian house. Not a hint of frivolity anywhere, but she refused to confess to the lack of it. "Remodeling this house—that's been fun."

Amanda rubbed her eyes sleepily. As he nestled the child comfortably in the crook of his arm, he raised his dark eyebrows above doubtful eyes and confronted her across the slumbering baby. "Sanding, scraping, painting—sounds like a barrel of laughs."

He was right to contradict her, but she'd never admit it—nor the reason his approval was so important to her. "Restoring this house has been very... satisfying."

He chuckled softly and shook his head. "So is mowing the lawn, but I'd never place it on my top ten list of things I enjoy."

Her defense had failed miserably, so she shifted to the offense. "What *is* on your top ten list?"

His expression turned thoughtful as he leaned back in the chair, rocking gently. "A quiet evening at home with a good mystery novel or video heads the list."

"See," she replied with satisfaction, "we're not that different."

The warmth of his smile radiated across the room. "I'm beginning to think we have a great deal in common."

She tore her focus away from the heat in his steel gray eyes and fumbled with the fabric beside her. "What else is on your list?"

"Do you like surprises?"

His swift change of subject threw her bewildered senses into further confusion. "That depends on whether they're good or bad."

He rose without disturbing the dozing child, and she avoided his eyes, concentrating on a fleck of pale yellow paint above his left cheekbone.

"Will you trust me if I promise a good surprise?" he asked in a teasing tone.

Her mouth went dry and her heart hammered at the sight of the powerful man, smiling down at her as he cradled the baby in his arms. Trust him? The way she felt at that moment, she'd follow him to the ends of the earth and back again at the crook of his little finger. What was the matter with her? What had happened to her good common sense Aunt Bessie had so often praised? Everything between them was an act, with Colin trying to please his father to keep him well, and her working to fulfill her contract with the syndicate and find Amanda a home.

Unable to speak, she nodded.

"Good." He passed Amanda to her. "I'll pick you up in an hour. We're going out to dinner."

"But Amanda—"

"I've already arranged for Mrs. Kaplan to stay with her."

Events were progressing too fast, and the idea of an evening out with Colin—alone—sent her head spinning. She rose to her feet and tried to center her whirling thoughts on her responsibilities. "What if the kidnapper—"

He placed his hands on her shoulders and slid them lightly down her arms, making her skin tingle beneath his touch. "I've taught Mrs. Kaplan how to activate the alarm system. She and Amanda will be fine."

"But—"

"No buts accepted. I'll see you in an hour for lesson number one in enjoying yourself." He moved his hands back up her arms, grasped her shoulders and pulled her to him, crushing her lips with his own.

I'm enjoying myself now. She struggled against the weakness in her knees to remain standing.

The kiss ended too soon. He drew away and ran a knuckle down the curve of her chin. "One hour. Wear something casual. We're going on a picnic."

She sucked in the breath his kiss had driven from her lungs. "A picnic? At night?"

He turned at the door and threw her a grin that sent a rush of pleasure from her head to her feet. "Learn to relish the unexpected—like that sweet bundle Farnsworth sent you. That's the best way to enjoy yourself."

Before she could think of an appropriate reply, the front door closed behind him.

COLIN TOOK the front steps two at a time, five minutes earlier than he'd promised. His heart was as light as his step when he rang the bell. Betsy, his favorite sister, had arrived, and his father seemed to be mending, looking and acting like his old self.

And his father wasn't the only one improving. For the first time since the divorce, the hollow, leaden feeling that had dragged him down had completely disappeared, and the bitterness that had corroded his insides every time he thought of Felicia had receded. He wondered if his improvement was due to time and distance between him and his ex-wife or the healing influence of Devon Clarke.

Damn. His very thoughts were betraying him now. Bad enough that his old man had shoved him hard in a direction he had no inclination to travel.

"Be nice to the girl," his father had begged him earlier in the day. "She's working herself silly, caring for an infant and preparing her house for the interview. She's going to crack if she doesn't take a break."

"A break?"

"Get her out of the house. Show her a good time. You could use some relaxation yourself," his father added. "Seems to me you've done nothing but work since you and Felicia separated."

"I'm a carpenter, not a dating service," he'd replied, dismissing the entire idea until he'd seen the pain on his father's face and noted the way he labored for breath. He wouldn't be responsible for upsetting his father and precipitating more heart trouble. He eased his father into a chair. "Whatever you say, Dad. Maybe a night out would do us both good."

He'd brought up the subject at lunchtime with his father as witness to ease the old man's worries. But Colin hadn't planned on enjoying the prospect of dating Devon.

When she opened the door to greet him, she was dressed in jeans that hugged her slender hips and a form-fitting white cotton top with the sleeves of a plaid shirt tied around her shoulders. The sight of her heart-shaped face, her cheeks flushed pink and her eyes bright with anticipation made his heart lurch dangerously.

"Let me say goodbye to Amanda," she said.

He followed her to the family room, where Mrs. Kaplan was ensconced in the rocker with her knitting on her lap.

"I brought out the portable crib, so Mrs. Kaplan won't have to climb the stairs to put Amanda to bed." Devon leaned into the playpen and picked up the child, and Amanda's tiny arms twined around her neck as Devon planted kisses on her cheeks. "Be a good girl for Mrs. K., kiddo."

The homey picture generated a longing deep within him, but he resisted the urge to collect them both into his arms and claim them as his own. Although beginning to heal, the wounds from Felicia were still too fresh, his judgment still unreliable. Life was too short for him to make another great mistake, and Devon hadn't indicated she'd changed her mind about putting the child up for adoption. For all he knew, she considered Amanda no more than a pleasant diversion, a responsibility she'd soon reject without a qualm.

The possibility of such an action on her part unsettled him. He'd allowed one woman who didn't want a family to break his heart. *Fool me once, shame on you. Fool me twice, shame on me.*

He wanted to turn on his heel and beat a speedy retreat before his untrustworthy emotions and his raging hormones mired him in a situation he wasn't prepared to accept, but memories of his father's face, pinched with pain, crossed his mind. A promise was a promise.

He squelched his misgivings and shifted his attention to the tiny, gray-haired woman counting stitches as she rocked. "Thanks for filling in on such short notice."

"My pleasure," Mrs. Kaplan said. "Now don't worry about a thing. Just have a good time. If I get sleepy, I'll stretch out on the sofa, so don't hurry home on my account."

With reluctance written clearly across her pretty features, Devon lowered Amanda into her playpen and turned worried eyes on him. "What if there's a problem? Where can Mrs. Kaplan reach us?"

His spirits lifted at her concern—a good sign. Felicia would have waltzed out the door without a backward glance. He patted his shirt pocket. "Mrs. Kaplan has my cell phone number. Ready to go?"

At the curb, he grasped her elbow as she climbed into the pickup. The smoothness of her skin, the subtle fragrance of her perfume, her tiny waist he could span with two hands and the grace of her long legs as she stepped into the cab sent his senses whirling.

While he circled the truck to the driver's side, he drew a deep breath to clear her tantalizing scent from his nostrils and the desire to make love to her right there on the sidewalk from his heart.

After settling behind the wheel and starting the engine, he grabbed the steering wheel and gave silent thanks for the covered picnic basket on the seat between them that forced him to keep his distance. Before he'd ever consider loving her, he had to know more about Devon Clarke, had to convince himself she wanted the same things he did—that home and family would always come before her career, before anything else. So far he had no proof of anything but the opposite.

"What's that heavenly aroma?" she asked. "It's making my mouth water."

As he put the truck into gear, he inclined his head toward the picnic basket. "Part of the surprise."

She smiled with a sweetness that burned her image into his mind. "I'm beginning to like this already."

"Ma'am," he replied with a Texas twang as he reached behind him for a Stetson he'd brought for the occasion, "you ain't seen nothin' yet."

Devon leaned back in the seat and turned her eyes to the road. He'd promised her a good time and nothing more, she reminded herself, and she shouldn't read anything else into their situation. He'd made himself perfectly clear about what he expected in a wife, and she was even less qualified than Felicia to fill that role. She'd enjoy the time she could spend with him and not expect more. To assume their relationship could ever be anything other than just friendly wouldn't be fair to either of them. She attempted to ignore the pang in her heart that that knowledge created.

He tuned in to a country station on the radio, and his strong, slender fingers tapped the wheel in time with the music. He headed the pickup into the city, then turned toward the bay.

"Do you dance?" he asked without taking his eyes from the road.

"Not recently," she hedged, ashamed to admit she hadn't tripped the light fantastic since the senior prom. *Tripped*, that was the word, all right. She didn't know whether to giggle or cry, remembering her two left feet with minds of their own.

"Don't worry," he assured her with a crooked smile. "It'll all come back as soon as you hear the music. You never forget. It's like—"

"Riding a bicycle? That's a relief." She endeavored to keep the skepticism from her voice. At age six, she'd given up learning to cycle after endless skinned knees and elbows and a broken wrist.

"We're here." He swung the truck into a parking lot that overlooked the bay, where the sun plunged beneath the horizon like a lozenge of liquid fire. Cars jammed the area, and people streamed toward a grassy park beside the water. He hooked the picnic basket over one arm and offered her the other as she stepped down from the cab.

She eyed the bandstand in the distance. "What's happening here?"

He grabbed a small cooler and a blanket from the truck bed and fell in step beside her as they followed the crowd. "A country fair."

"In the middle of the city?"

He drew in a deep breath as if testing the air. "That's the beauty of it. You can smell the sawdust and cotton candy from here. We'll find a spot near the bandstand and spread our picnic. Three of the hottest bands out of Nashville are playing tonight."

His enthusiasm infected her with a reckless exhilaration. "Sounds like fun."

"That's the spirit." He broke his stride and beamed at her. "I'll make a wild woman of you yet."

His words struck her with a bolt of truth. Something about Colin O'Reilly reached deep into the core of her, filling her with an unrestrained joy and the desire to break the prim mold of existence her life with Aunt Bessie had forged. She'd had no experience with love and felt like a diver poised on the edge of a high cliff for a plunge that would send her either into deep, unfamiliar waters or smashing onto rocks.

She fought against her powerful impulses, hanging back from the edge of love, afraid to commit to the leap needed to love him without reservation. "I thought you liked sedate domestic goddesses, not tigresses."

He spread the blanket across a grassy space close enough to hear the band, but far enough away to talk above the music. He settled cross-legged and reached out to pull her down beside him. "Domestic goddess by day, provocative temptress by night. A great character for a television series, don't you think?"

She lowered herself next to him, stretched her legs before her and leaned back on her elbows. She was tumbling off the precipice into love, whether she wanted to or not, and nothing could stop her. "What would you call this character?"

He reached into the cooler for a couple of beers, twisted off the caps and handed her one. "How about Wonder Wife?"

"Works for me." She drank a long sip of the icy brew, hoping to hide the way her pulses pounded at his suggestion. "And who would play her?"

"Interested in auditioning?" A significance she couldn't decipher lay beneath his light tone.

"You've gotta be kidding." She turned her face into the breeze off the bay, hoping its coolness would draw the heat from her cheeks. "I'm doubly unqualified, deficient in both domesticity and seduction."

"Don't sell yourself short." He leaned toward her until his lips were inches from hers. "Maybe you have talents you haven't discovered."

"Maybe I'm a realist." His arms rested on either side of her, trapping her in his embrace. If he kept looking at her that way, she was going to throw her arms around him and kiss him senseless right in front of the whole world. She had to extricate herself before she did or said something they'd both regret.

"Colin." She widened her eyes and gazed at him with what she hoped passed for innocence. "May I ask a question?"

His head dipped closer, and his breath caressed her face. "Anything."

"What's for supper? I'm starving."

His sharp bark of surprised laughter startled her, and she splashed her beer across the blanket. He sat back on his heels, pulled a checkered napkin from the picnic basket and mopped up the spill. "Do you know what I like about you, Devon?"

She scrambled a safe distance across the blanket. "You've never said you did."

He stared at her, brows drawn in confusion, the napkin suspended in midair. "Did what?"

The blush started at the roots of her hair and traveled to the neck of her tee. "Like me."

He dabbed again at the damp spot, studying it with a concentration that seemed forced. "No, I guess I never have said that I like you."

She longed to hear him speak the words, but he simply tossed the napkin aside, pulled the basket toward him and began extracting items from its depths.

"What I like about you—" he handed her a plate "—is that you're always surprising me."

Pleasure spread through her as she removed the lid from a container of potato salad and scooped a mound onto his plate. "Is that good?"

"Being surprised?" He opened a box of fried chicken and selected a plump drumstick. "Sure as hell beats being bored to death."

She searched the box for a chicken breast, unable to meet his eyes. Her heart thumped at her own audacity as she framed her question. "Was Felicia full of surprises?"

He tore into the drumstick with even white teeth and chewed with a reflective expression.

When he didn't answer, she fumbled with an apology. "Sorry, it's none of my business—"

"No, it's okay." His expression altered as if a thought had suddenly hit him. "I'm finally beginning to understand why my marriage failed."

She wasn't sure she liked the direction of the conversation, so she chose her words carefully. "You said before that you and Felicia had different goals...."

"We did." He set his plate aside and stared out across the water undulating with a mesmerizing rhythm against the base of the nearby seawall. As a black skimmer swooped low over the water's edge, the mango afterglow of sunset illuminated the strong planes of Colin's face. "Until just a few minutes ago, I blamed Felicia for everything."

"I don't understand." Her heart plummeted at the implication that he still loved his former wife.

"Just now, while I was talking with you, I made a discovery about myself, something that hit me like a blast out of nowhere." His eyes shone golden in the sunset's fading rays. "There's a word for that kind of discovery...."

"An epiphany?" Confusion raged within her when he lifted her hand and pressed his lips to her palm.

"That's it." He turned toward her with a somber look in his eyes. "For the first time, I saw *how* my marriage went wrong—and that its failure was my fault."

Her spirits dropped further at his admission, and she steeled herself for the announcement that he would return to Felicia to try again.

"Your talk of surprises made me understand," he added.

Her head swam as she attempted to follow his logic. "You've really lost me this time."

He shifted behind her on the blanket and drew her against his chest until they sat like nesting spoons, watching the sunset colors fade in the deepening twilight. "Felicia *never* surprised me. In retrospect, I can see she never changed. From the beginning, she gave every indication just how important her career was to her, how family and children would always come second."

"But you said—"

"I know, I accused her of changing. But now I realize I was always projecting my expectations on her, viewing her as the person I wanted her to be, not who she really was."

He held her firmly around her midriff with his forearm pressed just beneath her heart, and she wondered if he gauged its frantic tempo. She leaned against the warm hardness of his chest. "Does this epiphany of yours mean you and Felicia will get back together?"

"God, no." His words exploded in her right ear as he pressed his face against her hair. "Don't you see? Now that the bitterness is gone, I'm free."

She twisted in his arms to face him. "Free?"

He took her face between his palms and emotion swelled inside her. "Free to love again."

He kissed her deeply until a burst of applause drew them apart in embarrassment. She laughed with him as they realized the ovation was not for them, but the band that had completed its first number on the amphitheater stage.

"Come on." He rose to his feet and pulled her up beside him. "Let's join the group down front for some boot-scootin' boogying."

The evening passed in a blur of music and magic. Beneath the dark canopy strewn with stars, Devon danced, following Colin's easy lead as if she'd Texas-two-stepped all her life. Later, along the arcade of booths assembled for the weekend fair, they played games and stuffed themselves with sticky cotton candy and sugary bear claws.

"How about having our fortunes told?" Colin asked as they worked their way back through the sawdust aisles toward the parking lot.

"Try your skill at target shooting," a nearby barker called from his booth. "Win a prize for the little lady."

"Should I?" Colin asked.

"Maybe I should get back to Amanda." As perfect as the evening had been, she had registered the child's absence as a small empty space in her heart.

"This won't take but a minute." Colin peeled a few dollars from his wallet and accepted a pellet gun from the proprietor with a pockmarked face.

"Three hits inside the center ring and any prize in the house is yours," the man promised.

Colin extended the gun in his right hand and rested the butt in the palm of his left. With expert precision, he placed the first two shots in the center ring.

"Colin O'Reilly!" a voice behind her exclaimed. "I haven't seen you in eons."

Colin flinched, missing his last shot. He returned the gun to its owner and turned to face the woman who had ruined his aim. "Lisa Warner, isn't it?"

The plump young woman with flaming red hair and a liberal dusting of freckles smiled and gestured to the miniature reproduction of herself who clung to her hand. "I'm Lisa Paris now, and this is my daughter, Erin."

He smiled at the little girl before returning his attention to her mother. "Last time I saw you was high school graduation."

Lisa groaned. "Don't remind me. I'm already feeling ancient with three kids. The boys are with their father, riding bumper cars."

At Devon's discreet cough, he turned and pulled her arm through his. "This is Devon—"

"Nice to meet you," Devon blurted with a quickness that startled him.

Lisa's glance was friendly but curious. "I'd heard Colin was married. So you're the lucky woman."

"No—" The swift jab of Devon's elbow in his ribs interrupted him.

"No?" Lisa's eyes glimmered with interest.

"No," he improvised, "I'm the lucky one. It's been nice seeing you again, Lisa."

Lisa ignored his effort at dismissal. "Do you have children?"

"No—" he began, but Devon's elbow slammed his rib cage again.

"Not children," she smiled sweetly. "Just one little girl, Amanda. She's six months old."

"They're so precious at that age." Lisa looked ready to launch into a discourse on the attributes of babies, but the toddler yanked on her hand.

"Go potty, Mama," the little girl whined.

Lisa swung around, searching the midway.

Devon pointed toward the bandstand. "Rest rooms are over there."

"Thanks." Lisa scooped up the girl and headed off at a trot, calling over her shoulder. "We should all get together sometime."

As soon as Lisa had cleared out of earshot, Colin turned on the woman beside him. A shadow of amusement flitted across her face, but she said nothing.

"What the hell was that all about?" he asked.

She stood her ground, unblinking in the face of his disapproval. "We have a deal, remember?"

"My deal was for the interview, period." He shoved his hands in the back pockets of his jeans to keep from strangling her. His sense of being manipulated brought back all his bad memories of a marriage gone sour. "I didn't agree to play hubby for the duration."

"Nobody asked you to," she snapped. "Just do your part until the interview has aired—and don't blow my cover in the meantime. That's all I ask."

"All? That's a mighty tall order."

"If you're not up to it, tell me now. Don't back out on me at the last minute." Her eyes flashed and her jaw froze with determination.

For two cents he'd walk away and leave her standing there to find someone else to help save her precious career and honor her contract with her bloody syndicate.

She turned her back on him, jerked a fistful of dollars from her jeans and plunked them down before the pock-faced man. ''My turn.''

She grabbed the pellet gun, addressed the target and pulled off three quick shots, all dead center.

Colin's jaw gaped. ''Where did you learn to shoot like that?''

She returned the gun and thrust her chin in the air. ''Aunt Bessie taught me.''

''Hey, mister,'' the carny taunted him, ''ain't you gonna claim the prize your girlfriend won for you?''

God, she was one plucky woman. No wonder his father was so fond of her. He pointed to a huge pink teddy bear. ''This isn't my girlfriend,'' he said with dignity. ''She's my wife. And I'll take the stuffed animal for our daughter.''

Her head snapped up and her hazel eyes misted with tears. ''Thank you.''

He tucked the huge bear under one arm and threw his other around her shoulders. Devon Clarke was one surprise after another, and he wondered how many more she'd spring on him before their little charade had run its course.

''Come on, Mrs. O'Reilly, I'm taking you home.''

Chapter Ten

A sense of family is very important to children.
It gives them not only a feeling of security and
belonging but helps establish their identities and
provides an anchor in an ever-changing world.
Amanda Donovan, *Bringing Up Baby*

"You're cutting this awfully close," Leona said.

Devon, dressed only in bustier and panties, glanced
at her agent in the mirror and applied her makeup.
"It's over two hours until sunset. I have plenty of
time."

Leona leaned back on her hands on the bed, spread
her long, gauzy skirt, a tropical print of muted pinks,
and adjusted her off-the-shoulder blouse of matching hot pink. Disks the color of watermelon pulp
dangled from her ears.

Devon suppressed a smile, remembering how she'd
instructed her agent simply to wear pink for the faux
wedding, forgetting Leona's inclination toward the
flamboyant.

Leona straightened the pink hibiscus tucked behind her ear. "I'm not talking about the wedding,

cupcake. I'm referring to the interview. Sara Davis will be here in five days."

Devon dusted her face lightly with a transparent powder, rose from her dressing table and pointed an index finger skyward. "Blame the Man Upstairs for the delay. I hadn't planned on a tropical storm canceling our beachfront ceremony last weekend."

"With the ceremony tonight, will the video be ready for Sara's interview?" Leona asked.

"Relax. The videographer promised there'd be days to spare."

"I'll relax," the older woman muttered, "after this interview's been taped and aired. One false step anywhere along the way and we both could lose our jobs."

Devon sighed and cleaned her hands on a tissue. "I don't want to jeopardize your job—or mine—but I'm more worried about Amanda."

Leona's scrutinizing gaze burned between her shoulder blades. "You've really fallen for the little angel, haven't you?"

She nodded. "Big mistake. Giving her up will be agony, but it's the best thing. My attorney is looking for adoptive parents."

"Ever consider keeping her?" Leona asked with what seemed deliberate casualness.

Devon picked up Aunt Bessie's silver-backed brush and yanked it through her hair, hoping to drive away the hurt in her heart with the painful attack on her unruly curls. "In my dreams. But I'm not equipped to be a parent."

"Nonsense." Leona scooted off the bed and retrieved the bridal gown hanging over the closet door. "All you need is love."

Devon grinned at her agent and friend. "You're showing your age. Isn't that the title of an old Beatles hit?"

"Uh-huh, but that doesn't make it any less true." Leona removed the dress from its hanger and held it high for Devon to slip over her head.

"Love is definitely needed—but also a father and family and parenting skills," Devon mumbled through the folds of fabric. "I love Amanda so much, I want her to have it all, even if that means I'll never see her again."

"With that much love—" Leona began.

"No, I can't risk the child's happiness or safety."

"Safety?"

"I told you about the kidnapping attempts." Devon fumbled with a hook caught in her hair. "Placing Amanda with a family in another part of the country, giving her a new identity, will protect her from her half uncle."

Leona's penciled eyebrows peaked above her curious eyes. "You're sure he's behind all this?"

"Who else would it be? According to Amanda's attorney, he's a worthless bum who'd love to get his greedy mitts on Amanda's trust fund."

"An attorney said that?"

Devon grinned. "That's a rough paraphrase of the legalese." Her expression sobered. "I don't want her uncle ruining Amanda's life." She thrust her arms through the short sleeves and turned toward the mirror while Leona closed the zippered back. The sight of her reflection drove the air from her lungs. "I look like a bride."

"That's the idea," her friend said with a grin. "The question is, do you *feel* like a bride?"

"How I feel won't show on the video." Devon bent down to tie the satin laces of her espadrilles, glad for a chance to hide her flaming cheeks.

"*Au contraire,* cupcake. If your expression at the wedding is anything like I witnessed when you looked at Colin during lunch today, the camera will document the stunning spectacle of a woman head over heels in love."

Devon crisscrossed the laces slowly to give herself time to recover. Leona didn't miss much. She'd only been in town a few hours, yet she'd already homed in on a fact Devon had tried to avoid for the past two weeks: she loved Colin O'Reilly.

She had fought against the feeling without success, hampered by his constant presence—especially his nights spent sleeping on the sofa in her family room. She'd known from the beginning his attention to her and Amanda had been initiated—mandated was a better word—by Mike, but the knowledge that Colin entertained her only to please his father did nothing to dampen her attraction to him.

He'd taught her how to laugh and play, something she'd forgotten when Aunt Bessie died. In the past two weeks, when their work on the house was finished for the day, they'd danced, played miniature golf, combed the beaches for shells, watched old movies and picnicked in secluded parks. Her face flushed anew at the memory of his kisses, of the warmth of his callused hands on her breasts, lighting fires deep in her abdomen, stoking a longing that only he could satisfy.

She tied the last lace, took a few tentative steps in the unfamiliar shoes and adjusted the Battenberg lace collar around her shoulders. The charade would soon be over. Colin, on the rebound from Felicia, would complete the renovations on the old Victorian, go through with the interview and exit her life forever.

She remembered how he'd projected his expectations of a wife onto Felicia, seeking the qualities he longed for where none existed. Obviously, he'd done the same with her, and while he hinted they might have a future together, she was all too aware of her innate deficiencies as both lover and mother to allow him to entangle himself in another self-deception.

She stared at her reflection, noting her too-wide eyes and heated cheeks, while Leona fastened the circlet of silk daisies on her curls and arranged the satin streamers down her back.

Make the best of this wedding, she admonished herself. *It's the only one you'll ever have.*

"All set?" Leona asked.

Devon nodded, and with a curious mixture of anticipation and dread, followed her downstairs.

Colin, stunning in his gray tux, stood in the hallway. She had never seen him wearing anything other than jeans or a swimsuit, and the sight of him, looking coolly elegant yet ruggedly masculine, in spite of the sissy pink cummerbund, tightened her throat and created a strange prickling behind her eyelids.

Leona made a clucking sound with her tongue. "You shouldn't be here. It's bad luck for the groom to see the bride before the wedding."

"Don't be silly, Leona." Devon forced the words past the constriction in her throat and threw Colin a falsely bright smile. "This isn't a real wedding, and I'm not a real bride."

Colin said nothing, but observed her with an awe usually reserved for religious miracles or forces of nature. His expression told her things she wasn't ready to acknowledge.

Leona took one look at him and scurried toward the family room. "I'll check on the baby and Mrs. Kaplan."

Left alone with him, Devon fidgeted beneath his scrutiny. "Is something wrong?"

He held out his hand, and she stepped down the stairs toward him, feeling self-conscious and foolish in her blushing-bride costume.

"Something's missing."

His rich voice reverberated through her, sending her nerve endings humming, reawakening the longing deep in her core. Then the meaning of his statement hit her, generating a flutter of panic deep in her stomach. "Don't tell me I've forgotten something. I studied the column I wrote about the wedding and double-checked every detail."

"Don't worry." His smile lit the planes of his face, softening the angle of his jaw. "You've covered everything in the column."

"Then what—" Her voice broke with surprise as he turned and lifted flowers from a box on the hall table.

"Every bride should have flowers." He extended the bouquet toward her. "These weren't in your column, so I tried to guess what you might have chosen."

The old-fashioned bouquet of daisies, Queen Anne's lace, creamy white roses and fragrant buds of stephanotis, with satin ribbons tied in loveknots, perfumed the hall. She buried her face in the flowers, inhaling their luxurious scent while she marshaled her errant heart. His gesture was merely thoughtful, a detail she had overlooked, and she'd be a sentimental fool to read more into it.

She raised her head and smiled, careful not to betray her emotions in her expression. "Thank you. These are the perfect touch." Anxious to escape the charged atmosphere, she started down the hall toward the family room when a thought hit her, and she turned back to him. "I didn't order you a boutonniere."

"No problem." He reached into the mass of green tissue that had held her flowers. "One came with the bouquet, but I'll need your help to pin it on."

His eyes, dangerous as swirling mist, reflected an emotion that scared her senseless. She wanted to run to the safety of Leona and Mrs. Kaplan in the bright, sunny family room, but his gaze held her fast in the muted light of the hall, where dust motes danced in the rays of sunlight filtering through the leaded glass of the front door, creating an ethereal atmosphere of unreality.

When she slipped her hand behind his lapel to anchor the white rosebud backed with a sprig of fern, her fingers registered the dangerous thudding of his heart. Keeping her eyes on the pleated white expanse of his linen shirt, she secured the flower with a florist's pin.

Before she could retreat, he reached around her, pulling her toward him with one firm hand on the small of her back, the other tangled in the satin streamers at the nape of her neck. Through the delicate fabric of her gown, his body heat seared the length of her as his lips claimed hers.

Dizzy from the warmth of him, the intoxicating aroma of roses and stephanotis, and the shimmering light, she fought to remain objective.

None of this is real. It's only make-believe, her frantic mind assured her.

But her heart sang with the pressure of his lips and the taste of him on her tongue, and she arched against him, standing on tiptoe to deepen the kiss and press against the firm muscles of his chest.

The chime of the grandfather clock in the entryway broke the spell. She twisted away, breathless. ''We'll be late.''

He grinned with a languid movement of jaw and muscles that turned her bones to mush. ''Saved by the bell. Another minute and I'd have skipped the wedding altogether and cut straight to the honeymoon.''

Her thoughts dovetailed with his, and she thrust away the images those notions painted, dangerous fantasies that could lead only to heartache. With bustling efficiency, she gathered up her bouquet and smoothed her skirts.

"I'll ride with Leona in her rental car—" she avoided his eyes "—and meet you at Sunset Beach."

She retreated to the family room with her heart pounding so furiously in her ears, she didn't hear the door close behind him as he left.

LEONA TOOK THE TURN onto the beach causeway too fast, causing Devon to clutch the dashboard until her knuckles whitened. "No need to rush. We have plenty of time," she pleaded.

"Maybe for you." Leona pressed the accelerator, taking the bridge over the Intracoastal Waterway like a stuntman in an action movie's high-speed chase. "Any delays and I'll miss my plane. It leaves right after the ceremony."

"But I thought you were staying the night." Leona's departure would leave her alone with Colin, and after her encounter with him a few minutes earlier, their relationship had shifted onto a dangerous course. Now her friend would not be there to shield her from her own desires.

"I have an important meeting in New York first thing in the morning," Leona explained breezily. "Colin can drive you home."

The look of smug satisfaction on her friend's face indicated Leona had laid purposeful plans, but before Devon could accuse her, Leona screeched the car to a halt in the parking lot at the edge of Sunset Beach beside the caterer's van.

Beyond the dunes, the sounds of reggae music drifted to them on the sea breeze, and the crisp green-and-white stripes of a marquee jutted above the feathery tops of sea oats. As they crossed the wooden boardwalk that traversed the dunes, the sun sank low above the tranquil turquoise waters of the Gulf of Mexico.

"There's my former editor, Jake Blalock, who'll be our 'minister.'" Devon pointed to a tall, distinguished man in a dark navy suit. "And Mike and Betsy."

"And the groom has arrived." Colin came up behind her and slipped his arm through hers. "The videographer's unloading his equipment in the parking lot, and as soon as he's set up, we can get on with the show."

The warmth of his fingers on her arm sent a shiver of pleasure through her.

"You okay?" he asked.

She nodded. "Just nervous—and anxious for all this to be over."

"Me, too." A burning promise shone briefly in his eyes before his expression cleared. He clasped her hand in a reassuring squeeze. "There's nothing to be nervous about. You've planned for every conceivable circumstance. What could go wrong?"

She glanced around with dismay. "For starters, the tour bus hasn't arrived. We can't have a wedding without guests—the column mentioned a crowd of family and friends. And the sun will set in a few minutes."

"I didn't think you were the type to succumb to wedding jitters," he teased. "Take a look around. The caterers have set up the buffet, the potted palms and flowers are arranged above the surfline, ready to frame the wedding party, the guests' chairs are in place. When the bus arrives, we can begin in seconds."

She resisted the urge to chew her nails and concentrated instead on the videographer, setting up a stationary camera behind the rows of folding chairs. He swung another camera onto his shoulder and took a position near Jake Blalock, who waited between the palms with a prayer book in his hand. Betsy had taken a seat in the front row, and Mike stepped forward to act as best man.

"See," Colin said, pointing to the roof of a charter bus, visible above the dunes as it pulled into the parking lot. "Your guests have arrived with time to spare."

The chatter of excited voices drifted over the dunes from the parking lot, but Devon's concern now was with the sun, dangerously near setting before the ceremony even started. She turned her back on the boardwalk, only dimly registering the thud of footsteps as the tourists filled the chairs behind her.

"Here comes the bride." Colin's smile melted her heart as he offered his arm, and everything around her except the handsome man at her side faded into nothingness.

The band modulated into a New Age bridal march as Devon took Colin's arm and walked toward Jake. Leona and Mike fell in behind them.

Devon felt she was moving in slow motion through a dream. She glanced at Colin's rugged profile, tanned and self-assured above his stiff white collar and the broad shoulders of his gray tux. In all her wildest fantasies, she couldn't have imagined a more perfect groom, a man who could stir her senses more, one who inspired such confidence and trust. If this were real, she'd have a lifetime ahead to spend with him, to revel in his company, share his joys and sorrows, be comforted by his presence, sustained by his love.

But the wedding wasn't real. As storybook perfect as the setting was, with the sun splashing beneath a corona of luminous apricot into the teal blue sea, as handsome and exciting as Colin appeared, the ceremony was only make-believe. Despite that knowledge, Jake's words brought tears to her eyes.

"Dearly beloved," he intoned from the Book of Common Prayer, "we are gathered together to join this man and this woman in holy matrimony..."

Jake paused, and Devon tore her attention from Colin to her former editor, staring wide-eyed and open-jawed past her toward the audience.

"What is it?" she hissed nervously. She stopped herself from looking behind her, knowing the camera would record her distraction.

Beside her, Leona's shoulders shook with suppressed laughter.

With a subtle shake of his head to indicate all was well, Jake closed his mouth and resumed the ceremony. The familiar words of the wedding liturgy rose and fell with the rhythm of the waves, a flock of laughing gulls wheeled past in the dwindling sunlight, and the sultry tropical breeze kissed her cheeks like a blessing. Her hand, tightly clasped in Colin's strong fingers, registered the pounding of his blood, mingling its beat with hers until the two hearts pulsated as one. Reality receded, and she was no longer playacting. She embraced the fantasy, the wonder of the moment.

She lifted her eyes to Colin's as he slipped a simple gold band on her finger and, with all her heart, pledged eternal love to the man before her, while her reason, held prisoner by the magic around her, remained silent.

"With this ring, I thee wed." Colin's burning eyes reflected the glow of her love, and her knees threatened to buckle beneath the intensity of his gaze.

"You may now kiss the bride," Jake announced.

Colin cradled her face between his warm, callused palms and pressed his mouth to hers, and she tasted the salt spray from the breeze on his lips. Behind her, a soft sigh of appreciation from the watching tourists penetrated the fog of happiness in her brain.

"Ladies and gentleman," Jake continued in his best ministerial imitation, "may I present Mr. and Mrs. Jeffrey Donovan."

At the sound of their pseudonyms, she broke free of the magical spell, and her heart ached with loss.

It's only make-believe. Putting on a brave face, she turned with Colin to greet their guests.

Before her eyes could focus in the gathering twilight, dozens of flashbulbs exploded, blinding her momentarily. Unable to see, she moved forward, relying on the pressure of Colin's hand beneath her elbow to steer her down the aisle between the chairs toward the marquee.

"I'm starved," Colin whispered in her ear, and his words were heavy with a double meaning that echoed in her own heart.

He led her into the marquee behind a linen-draped table that held a five-tiered cake topped with enormous butterflies of delicate spun sugar. Champagne corks popped, and someone thrust a glass into her hand.

The guests crowding into the tent and settling at the tables drew none of her attention. She had eyes only for Colin, who saluted her with his champagne flute held high.

"To my darling wife," he said with an unfamiliar huskiness in his voice. "Lasting love and long life."

She lifted her glass to his and clinked it gently. *Make-believe,* she reminded herself, drawing her gaze from the heat in his eyes. She raised her glass to her lips and shifted her glance to the audience before her.

Before a second barrage of flashbulbs exploded, she registered for the first time a sea of smiling faces. *Asian* faces.

While she watched in stunned disbelief, the videographer moved among the crowd, documenting her "family and friends," a congenial group of Japanese tourists.

Chapter Eleven

Like love, rituals and traditions are the glue that
holds a family together. It is never too early to
begin building those occasions that create a
sense of belonging and continuity for your baby
as he or she grows and develops.

Amanda Donovan, *Bringing Up Baby*

Devon choked on her champagne, and Colin
pounded helpfully between her shoulder blades.

"Are you okay?" He took her glass and patted her
chin with a linen napkin.

"My God," she gasped when she could draw
breath. "They're all *Asians*."

"Tsk, tsk, Mrs. Donovan, your prejudice is showing." He grinned to soften his words. "This is supposed to be the happiest moment of your life, so
you'd better ditch that scowl and smile for the camera."

Her face contorted in a forced smile. "That camera can't do me a heck of a lot of good right now.
Only a village idiot would believe this group, friendly
and pleasant as they appear, are *my* kith and kin."

God, but she was adorable when she squirmed like that. "I warned you about deception."

"Too late. I'm up to my neck in it now." Her smile crumpled.

He leaned toward her, nuzzling the soft skin of her neck as he whispered in her ear, "I'll see what I can do."

He welcomed the chance to withdraw from her presence, to break the magic spell she'd cast on him since the moment she'd descended the stairs dressed in the white bridal gown that skimmed her firm breasts and slim waist and offered a provocative glimpse of her bare, tanned ankles.

On the opposite side of the crowded marquee, he cornered the photographer for a brief exchange of words, then threaded his way back through the filled tables to Devon.

"Everything's taken care of," he assured her. "The cameraman will avoid any frontal views of the guests, and he promises to edit out any of the tourists' faces he's already shot."

Her expression shifted from one of despair to hopefulness. "Won't that look odd?"

He tucked her arm through his and led her toward the dance floor as the happy guests crowded around them. "We'll explain to Sara Davis that we had a fire in the house that damaged portions of the video."

She stopped so abruptly he stepped on her toe. She rolled her eyes skyward and smacked him hard on the upper arm. "*Now* you think of it. We could have told her the fire destroyed the *entire* film and avoided this whole charade."

With her eyes blazing with reflected candlelight, her cheeks flushed and the off-the-shoulder collar of her dress revealing the silken skin of her shoulders, she filled him with a protectiveness and longing he'd never known. No bride had ever looked more radiant. Not even Felicia in the first heady flush of their relationship had affected him as Devon did now with her fresh, natural beauty and spunky personality.

He drew her into his arms for the bridal waltz. "I'm glad I didn't think of it because, Mrs. Donovan, I wouldn't have missed this for the world."

DRIVING HOME LATER that evening, he sighed with contentment, remembering the curve of Devon's hip against his own as she sliced the beribboned knife into the wedding cake, the laughter in her eyes when she fed him the first bite, the lightness of her in his arms as they danced to the reggae band. Even after she'd partnered a dozen or more of their honored Japanese guests, her animation hadn't dimmed.

He chuckled, recalling the impromptu "family" portrait, made up of Leona, his dad and Betsy and five of the waiters and waitresses from the catering company pressed into emergency duty. If Devon's earlier misgivings about the ceremony still bothered her, she'd hidden them well, behaving like the happiest bride on earth while she mugged for the camera.

She'd been quiet ever since she'd tossed her bouquet to a delighted young Japanese woman as they pulled away from the beach in a shower of confetti and politically correct birdseed. She sat staring out

the side window of his pickup, and all he could see of
her face was the delicate line of her cheek. A vein
pulsed lightly beneath a satin streamer that rested
against the slim column of her neck. When he pulled
in front of her house, he realized her shoulders were
shaking.

"Devon, don't cry."

He slid over and pulled her into his arms, tucking
her head beneath his chin, holding her close while he
stroked her soft curls and ran his fingers along her
shoulder blades. She made a tiny, muffled noise, and
his heart wrenched at the sound of her unhappiness.
He had thought she'd accepted the unexpected Japanese invasion with good grace, but evidently it had
upset her more than he'd realized.

"Everything will be fine," he consoled her. "You'll
see when you've viewed the video."

At his words, her shoulders shook harder and she
buried her face against his shirt as if to stifle her cries.
Then, gasping for air, she threw her head back—
laughing. Tears streamed down her face.

Between his relief and the infectious nature of her
giggles, he couldn't resist and found himself joining
her, howling with laughter.

"Can you imagine—" she sucked in air "—Sara
airing the unedited video on national television?
People would think they'd tuned in to some screw-
ball comedy series."

"Food—and family—catered by Benihana's." He
pulled a handkerchief from his pocket and handed it
to her.

While she wiped her tears and blew her nose, he reveled in the wondrous physical release of a good laugh. He hadn't laughed like that in years. The weight of guilt, discontent and a thousand regrets lifted from his shoulders, and for the first time since three years ago, when he'd first realized his marriage to Felicia had been irretrievably broken, he felt totally free of bitterness, whole of heart.

He escorted Devon, still hiccuping with laughter, inside, where she rushed straight to Amanda's portable crib in the family room.

"She's been no trouble at all," Mrs. Kaplan assured her. "Slept the entire time you were gone."

Devon gathered the sleeping child into her arms and pressed the baby's plump cheek to her face. "I'll take her up to her bed—in her own room now, thanks to Colin's hard work."

The sight of them, a beautiful Madonna in white and her slumbering child, stabbed him with a poignance that was painful in its potency. He blinked away moisture gathering in his eyes, offered his arm to Mrs. Kaplan and cleared his throat to speak. "I'll walk you home." A few minutes later, when Devon descended the stairs, Colin stood in the hall, removing his coat. He unfastened the pink cummerbund, tossed it atop his tux jacket with a gesture of disgust and raised his smoky gaze to hers. "The things I do for you, Devon Clarke."

The undisguised passion in his eyes sent her heart pounding like a steel drum. "I haven't told you often enough that I'm grateful," she murmured huskily.

As she stared at him, the spacious entryway seemed to shrink, and her lungs couldn't draw enough air. She read a sensual heat in his look but couldn't form the words or movements to dissuade him. The wedding, perhaps even the love that shone in his eyes, was make-believe, but she'd already accepted the fantasy as all she'd ever have. She hadn't the resolve to deny herself any part of that small compensation.

When he stepped toward her and scooped her in his arms, she twined her arms around his neck and laid her head against his shoulder with a contented sigh. Tomorrow, reality might crash in on her again, but tonight she'd dream.

She reveled in the strength of him as he carried her up the stairs and kicked open her bedroom door.

"A bride should be carried across the threshold for luck." Hoarse with emotion, his voice sounded in her ear.

Luck. She'd need a ton of it. She was even less prepared for this than she'd been for motherhood. Even if dear old Aunt Bessie had been inclined to explain about love between a man and woman, the confirmed old maid hadn't had a clue.

"I'm not really a bride." Devon had meant to protest, but her voice rose breathlessly, forming a question.

His arms tightened around her. "A more beautiful bride never existed."

When he released her and set her on her feet, her body slid the length of his, skimming his taut muscles and hard arousal. Desire blossomed deep within her, and she lifted her lips to him, welcoming his deep, probing kiss and the crushing pressure of his embrace.

Her body trembled, assaulted by surge after surge of emotion so powerful it stole her breath away. She broke clear from the sweetness of his kiss to gasp for air.

When he stepped away, every nerve ending in her body shuddered at the loss. His ragged breathing thundered in the stillness, and his gray eyes shone almost black in the dim light from the bedside lamp. "Do you want me to leave?"

Yes, her common sense screamed as she met his gaze head-on. "No."

With a reverent gesture, he lifted the circlet of daisies from her head and set it aside. He traced the planes of her face, the fullness of her lips, and brushed the sensitive skin of her throat with his fingertips before grasping her bare shoulders and swiveling her around.

All her senses sharpened. She detected the faint whir of the air-conditioner fan and felt its soft current against her flesh. In the dresser mirror, her reflection stared back at her, wide-eyed, dream-struck, with Colin behind her, etched sharply in the faint light, his gaze meeting hers in the mirror. Her mouth went dry with a strange mixture of fear and anticipation, and for the life of her, she couldn't tell if she feared he would leave—or he wouldn't.

"Colin." She breathed his name like a plea, unable to form a lucid thought other than being aware of his presence and her need.

"I love you, Devon." He dipped his head and covered her silky shoulders with tender, nibbling kisses that made her knees melt with desire, while he lowered the zipper on her dress and slid the sleeves down her arms until the soft white cotton bodice and skirt floated down into a cloud at her feet.

With a soft cry, she turned to him, wanting to return his declaration, but biting back the words. She would love him, make love with him, just this once, for memory's sake, but she would make no promises that would bind him in a disastrous mistake and make him regret her as he did Felicia.

She could hold back her words, but from his expression, she knew she'd failed miserably at keeping love and desire from shining in her eyes. The tenderness in his look turned her weak with longing.

He lifted her in his arms and carried her to the bed, lowering her gently on her back. With nimble fingers, he untied the satin laces of her espadrilles and tossed them aside before planting a kiss on the instep of each foot.

Without taking his gaze from hers, he deftly popped the studs from his pleated shirt and shrugged it off. The nimbus of light from the bedside lamp flickered and shifted, illuminating the tanned angles of his face and the powerful muscles of his chest and arms. His physical strength could have held her captive, had he wished, but it was the caring in his expression, more powerful than any physical force, that prevented her from following the dictates of reason and fleeing before it was too late.

Already it was too late. With a graceful gesture, he unhooked her bustier and threw it aside before cupping her breasts in his hands, sending a sensation of fiery pleasure throughout her body.

Ohhh, Aunt Bessie never told me about this.

He withdrew his hands, causing her breasts to ache with yearning, and sat on the edge of the bed, allowing her an intimate view of the wide expanse of his muscled back as he tugged off his shoes and socks. An image formed in her mind of bedtime every night for the rest of her life with the cozy presence of Colin, barebacked beside her, preparing for bed, their bed.

But then he stood, the rasp of a zipper sounded, and he stepped out of his pants and boxer shorts. Coziness swiftly evolved into excitement. Like a mythic Greek god, he stood naked before her, his broad shoulders tapering to his narrow waist. And at the juncture of those slender hips and powerful legs—Aunt Bessie had certainly never told her about *that*.

She should warn him that he was dealing with a total novice. "I don't—"

His mouth stopped her words as he straddled her, forcing her back into the pillows, and when he lifted his head from her lips and trailed kisses down her throat and across her breasts, her declaration of inexperience evaporated like drizzling rain on a hot summer sidewalk.

When he slipped his thumbs beneath the elastic of her panties and whisked them away, his gaze never left her face. The hard pewter of his eyes softened, reminding her of velvet kittens and cottony clouds of spring showers.

She reveled in the sensation of her bare flesh against his and wondered at her own lack of vulnerability. Feeling protected, cherished, she surrendered to him, sighing with delight as his mouth caressed her breasts. With gentle hands, he traced the contours of her rib cage, smoothed the curve of her hips and stroked the sensitive flesh of her thighs. When his fingers teased between her legs, sending waves of ecstasy through her in an explosion of sensation that erased every conscious thought, she feared she would die of pleasure.

She gripped the corded muscles of his shoulders as he tipped her hips and entered her with a sure, swift thrust. A brief pain preceded a burst of joy, then pleasure cascaded into deeper delight. He clasped her to him, and their bodies melded in a unity in which man and woman disappeared, and one creature, born of love, emerged.

Pleasure rocketed through her as time disappeared, their hearts pounded in concert, and their oneness transcended earth to soar among the stars.

Later, snuggled contentedly against him like a nesting spoon, with his arm clutching her midriff, her thoughts drifted in the twilight between consciousness and sleep.

Poor Aunt Bessie. She never knew what she missed.

DEVON SLEPT WITHOUT dreaming and awoke with Colin still asleep beside her on her pillow. She propped herself on her elbow and studied him, the angles of his face blurred with a stubble of beard, his dark lashes long against his cheeks, his tousled hair tumbling over his forehead. Her body ached with the delicious memory of their lovemaking the night before, and she added the image of his sleeping beside her to her store of memories, a treasure trove to covet through her long, lonely days.

Maybe dear old Aunt Bessie had been fortunate after all. She hadn't died little by little each day, yearning for what she'd lost.

Devon slid from beneath the covers, careful not to wake Colin. Her body, although sated and tender, encouraged her to continue where they'd left off last night, but in the cool, clear light of early morning, her head ruled, and she headed for the shower.

When she turned off the pulsing water, Amanda's cries carried through the wall of the bathroom. Devon tied on her robe, gave her hair a quick rub with a towel and, hoping to quiet the baby before she awakened Colin, padded down the hall to Amanda's room.

Amanda's wailing crescendoed as Devon opened the door, and she hastened to turn off the monitor to keep the child's racket from disturbing Colin.

Morning light filtered through the cheery yellow curtains and cast dappled shadows on the fabric sculptures of fairy-tale characters on the far wall and across the polished oak floor, but Amanda's disposition was far from sunny. The baby kicked and screamed, flailing the air with her fists as if she was mad at the world.

Devon struggled to change her diaper without skewering the tossing body, then cradled the still-sobbing child against her shoulder as she hurried to the kitchen to prepare the baby's breakfast.

While she fed a fretful Amanda her morning bottle, fantasies of the wedding and making love with Colin receded, and cold, hard reality gripped Devon once more. A *real* mother would know why her child was crying and how to make her stop. When Devon had visited attorney John St. Clair, she'd asked him to find Amanda parents who already had other children. The poor thing had lost her own parents and been stuck with Devon and all her inexperience. Amanda didn't need to suffer through basic training for parents a third time.

"Good morning, sunshine." Dressed in jeans and an unbuttoned shirt, Colin stood in the doorway, looking more handsome than any man had a right to. "Did you sleep well?"

Tell him, her conscience goaded her. *Let him know Amanda's leaving as soon as St. Clair finds her a home.*

But her heart rebelled, knowing Colin would walk out the door when he learned of the adoption. She couldn't tell him now, not because she feared ruining the interview and losing her syndicated column, but because she hoped for a few more days like yesterday, a few more nights like the one they'd just shared. Selfishly, she craved more memories to cache away, treasures to cherish when she was alone once again.

She smiled at him over Amanda's soft curls. "I slept fine. How about you?"

"Like a rock. I could get used to that." He sauntered into the kitchen and began making coffee.

So could I. She bit her lip, holding back the words. She wanted him to stay, to become a beloved habit in her life, but fate had ruled otherwise. Still, she could enjoy the short time left. Two weeks ago, St. Clair had said he would have some news for her within a month. At best, that left her two more weeks with Colin.

A comfortable silence, broken only by Amanda's sucking noises and the sizzle of pancakes Colin was cooking on the griddle, filled the room. She had expected to feel embarrassment, self-consciousness, after last night's passion, but instead she experienced only a gratifying contentment. She shared warm glances and secret smiles with him that spoke volumes as they ate breakfast and watched Amanda contentedly running a push toy across the floor of her playpen.

"Let's take our coffee into the living room," he suggested when they'd finished eating. "That's where the Davis crew will film most of the interview, so I'd better make a punch list to be sure we're ready."

Devon checked Amanda, who had curled on her side and gone back to sleep, before she followed Colin up the hall. Strong sunlight streamed through the eastern windows, and as she moved to adjust the curtains, a car parked at the curb down the block caught her eye.

"Colin, come look."

He stepped behind her, and she could feel the warmth of his breath on her hair as he peered down the street. His arms encircled her waist, and he drew her against him. "What am I supposed to be looking at?"

"That green Buick. I've seen it before." The sight of the car brought an involuntary shiver and a sense of uneasiness she couldn't explain.

"It's only an old car." He nibbled her ear playfully. "Probably belongs to one of the neighbors."

Rivers of desire coursed through her at his touch, banishing her anxiety. "If you keep that up, we'll never get around to that punch list."

He turned her to face him and buried his face in her neck. "Suits me."

"Oh, no, you don't." She longed to give in to him, to spend the morning as she'd spent the previous night, but the pressure of the interview and all that had to be done to make ready for it weighed down on her. Reluctantly, she pushed him away. "There're too many other things to do. We can't be—distracted."

"You, Mrs. Donovan, have driven me to distraction, so it's all your fault." He grabbed for her again, but she sidestepped nimbly.

"Maybe you'd better channel all that raging testosterone to your muscles," she teased, grinning at his expression of mock offense, "and help me lug the Christmas decorations down from the attic."

His offended expression deepened, but his eyes twinkled. "One way or another, I can see you only want me for my body."

"It has its uses," she quipped, heading for the stairs.

"Such as?"

She blushed, recalling the satisfaction he'd given her the night before. Pretending nonchalance, she leaned over the banister and peered through the open door of the family room. Amanda was sleeping peacefully in her playpen, nestled against a stuffed bunny.

Devon advanced up the stairs with her back to him. "Let's see," she said, beginning to tick items on her fingertips. "You're very good at lifting and toting heavy loads, sawing, hammering and nailing...."

He stopped beside her on the second floor, reached for the handle that lowered the attic stairs and flashed her a grin. "I'm good at nailing?"

She ignored his leer and climbed toward the attic, talking over her shoulder. "But I've forgotten to mention your greatest talent."

At the head of the attic stairs, he reached up and yanked the cord on the exposed lightbulb, flooding the dusty room with dim light. "I was beginning to think you didn't appreciate me. What have you recognized as my greatest skill?"

She crossed her arms and considered him with her most serious expression. "After a great deal of thought, I must admit it's the way you—"

"Yes?" He moved toward her with his eyes glowing dangerously.

"The way you handle a paintbrush." She stepped behind Aunt Bessie's dress form to avoid his grasp.

He reached behind the buxom shape and pulled her toward him. "A paintbrush, eh? Now you're giving me ideas."

She swallowed hard at his innuendo and pointed beneath the rafters. "There they are, the boxes marked Xmas."

"We'll save the paintbrushes for another time," he said with a mocking sigh. He turned toward the boxes she'd indicated and arched his eyebrows over disbelieving eyes. "There're *nine* of them."

She ignored her pounding heart and shrugged. "Christmas in this house is serious business."

"Then we'd better get started." He handed her the smallest box, then tucked one under each of his arms and sidled down the attic stairs.

After three more trips, all nine boxes were stacked in the living room, ready to be unpacked.

"You have enough stuff here to decorate three houses," he observed. "Where do you expect to put it all?"

"Most of it goes on the tree. The tree!" she said with a sense of rising alarm. "Where are we going to find a Christmas tree this time of year?"

He hauled her into his arms. "To prove to you I'm more than just a bundle of muscles, I'm about to dazzle you with my amazing network of friends."

She studied the cherished angles of his face as she leaned back in his arms and joined in the play. "I think I can take it. Dazzle me."

"My old high school pal, Duane Thomas, owns a farm outside of Brooksville that includes a few acres of Florida pines. We can drive up there this morning and cut one."

"That'll be fun," she said. "Amanda loves to ride. Maybe it will take her mind off her teething."

Amanda. Suddenly, the dread she'd experienced earlier at the sight of the green Buick surged back, and a cold premonition of disaster trickled down her spine.

"I'd better check on Amanda," she said. "She's been awfully quiet."

Propelled by fear, she raced to the family room and the playpen.

Her scream reverberated through the old Victorian. "She's gone. Amanda's gone!"

Chapter Twelve

Be prepared for the fact that the pain your child will bring you is proportional to the joy. The more you love your baby, the greater your distress if your child is injured or ill, but at such times, you must remain calm and think clearly for your baby's sake.

Amanda Donovan, *Bringing Up Baby*

Tears clung to Devon's long lashes and stained her pale cheeks as she mumbled incoherently in her sleep and thrashed her head against the pillow. Colin hoped she wouldn't awaken soon from the first rest she'd had in two days. He removed an afghan from the back of the sofa, adjusted the living room blinds against the late-afternoon sun and tiptoed quietly from the room.

His father and Betsy looked up from the table in the breakfast nook when Colin entered the family room.

"Is she asleep?" his father asked.

Colin nodded, trying to ignore the bone-wracking fatigue seeping through his body. He'd had only a couple hours sleep himself since Amanda had disappeared, and he was running now on caffeine and rage. He filled a mug with coffee and joined them at the table.

"Poor Devon." Betsy, who looked more like his mother with every passing year, patted his arm as his mother used to. "She's hardly slept at all—and neither have you. It's been two days and still no word."

Colin combed his fingers through his hair and rolled his head from side to side in an attempt to ease the tension in his shoulders. It seemed like two years, not two days, since he'd heard Devon's scream and rushed into the family room to find Amanda's playpen empty and the back door banging in the breeze.

"Any ransom request yet?" Betsy asked.

"No," Colin said. "No note or phone call."

The baby's laughing face, her big dark eyes, chubby cheeks and one-toothed grin filled his mind and twisted his heart with searing pain.

She'd been gone two days—and the more time that passed, the worse the prospects of ever seeing her alive, according to FBI special agent Stephen Wilcox, who'd set up shop in the dining room to monitor all incoming calls.

As if on cue, Wilcox, a slender young man in a suit and starched shirt, appeared in the doorway.

"Join us." Betsy waved him toward a seat at the table. "I'll pour you some coffee."

"Anything new?" Colin asked as he passed Wilcox the sugar bowl.

Wilcox accepted a mug of steaming coffee with a grateful smile and stirred in two heaping spoons of sugar. "Just got a call from our office in Kansas City. They've tracked down Ernest Potts and his wife."

"And?" Mike leaned forward, his blue eyes blazing.

"He owns a green Buick," Wilcox said.

Mike slapped the tabletop with his palm. "Then he's the one. For two cents, I'd bash his ugly face."

"Easy, Dad. Remember your heart." Colin recalled rushing out the back door when Devon discovered Amanda missing, but had found no sign of the child or the green Buick parked down the block earlier.

"Potts and his wife," Wilcox continued, "claim they haven't left Missouri during the past week. They were supercooperative, even insisted the agents search their house."

"Did they?" Colin asked.

"Yep." Wilcox drained his cup and set it aside. "They came up with *nada*."

Colin's heart ached for tiny Amanda and for Devon, prostrate with grief. "What now?"

Wilcox glanced toward the living room and lowered his voice. "I won't lie to you. The more time passes, the less the chance we'll find the baby—alive."

With a fist to her lips, Betsy stifled a sob.

"We're doing all we can." Taking his coffee cup, Wilcox rose to his feet. "I'd better get back to the phones."

Mike, looking gray and haggard, watched him go. "We're going to need a miracle to find that little sweetheart."

A miracle. An idea exploded in Colin's mind. "Dad, you're a genius."

His father threw him a puzzled look, and Betsy studied him through tear-glazed eyes, while Colin rummaged in the drawer beneath the telephone for the phone book, flipped it open and located the number for the *Courier.*

"What are you up to?" his father demanded.

"I'm asking for a media miracle." Colin punched the newspaper's number into the phone. "I'm calling Jake Blalock, Devon's former editor. If we can get Amanda's photograph in every newspaper in the country, maybe some reader will call in with a lead."

Betsy shook her head. "I don't mean to sound jaded, but children disappear every day all over the country. You'll be lucky to get a small write-up in the local paper—and maybe sooner or later a picture on a milk carton."

Colin covered the mouthpiece and grinned at his sister. "You forget that Amanda is the daughter of nationally syndicated baby expert, Amanda Donovan, whose column is carried by over four hundred newspapers in major cities all over the United States. If *her* baby is missing, that's major news for every one of those papers."

Mike rubbed his chin thoughtfully. "It's a long shot."

Colin's grin faded. "It's the *only* shot we have."

COLIN SAT IN THE DARKNESS, staring at the silhouette of the sofa where Devon was sleeping. Betsy and his father had gone home to supper an hour ago, and

Wilcox dozed by the extension phone in the dining room.

"What time is it?" Devon's voice, hoarse with tears, broke through the darkness.

He reached beside him and clicked on a table lamp that flooded the room with soft light. "Eight o'clock. Are you hungry?"

She shook her head, and her face took on a pinched expression that told him she was trying hard not to cry.

"You need to eat, to keep up your strength." He wanted to take her in his arms, make the hurt go away, and see her hazel eyes sparkle with laughter once again. Silently, he cursed his helplessness. "Mrs. Kaplan brought some homemade soup. Let me heat you some."

"I couldn't swallow." She glanced at the closed pocket doors of the dining room across the hall. "Has Wilcox—"

"Not a word—except that Potts is in Missouri, and Amanda isn't with him." He levered himself from his chair, crossed the room and sat beside her. He wanted to console her, to draw her into his embrace and share her hurt, but every muscle of her body, taut with grief, repelled his touch. He attempted to reassure her. "We may hear something soon. I talked with Jake Blalock, and he's sending the story and Amanda's picture to the wire services."

A glimmer of hope flickered across her face. "Surely someone's seen her. She couldn't have just vanished from the face of the earth." Horror replaced hope. "Unless—"

"We'll find her." He sounded more confident than he felt. "And she'll be fine."

"I never thought a house could feel so empty." She surveyed the room with a blank, forlorn stare. "She never made much noise—except when she needed changing or feeding, but the whole house echoes with silence now, as if she's filled it to the top with her presence."

He pulled her against his chest and stroked her hair, letting her talk, hoping words would ease her agony.

"I find myself listening for her babbling on the monitor." She nestled closer in his embrace, and he sensed a slight lessening of the tension in her body. "I look to her playpen or her crib, anticipating how her face lights up when she sees me. Every move I make draws my thoughts to her."

He pressed his lips against the smooth skin of her forehead. "That's because you love her."

She drew away and considered him, her eyes swimming with tears. "You're right. I never realized how much until now."

He stood and pulled her to her feet. "You haven't been out of the house in two days. Let's go get something to eat, even if it's only takeout to bring back with us."

She shook her head slowly, as if the simple movement was too much effort. "I have to stay here in case someone calls."

He observed her with a mixture of admiration and pain. "If I call Betsy to come answer the phone..."

Her head snapped up and her eyes lost their dull glaze. "If Potts isn't the one who took Amanda, it

has to be someone in the city. Ask Betsy to stay here
while you and I search for the green Buick.''

He hadn't the heart to remind her the police and
FBI had been canvassing the city for the past two
days. The important thing was to get her out of the
house, cajole her into eating something and possibly
take her mind off Amanda's absence for a few minutes.

"I'll make a deal," he offered. "You eat something, and I'll drive you wherever you want to go."

She set her mouth in a tight line, but her lower lip
trembled. Inwardly, he raged against his uselessness,
his inability to staunch her pain, to rescue Amanda,
to protect the two he loved like his own family.

At first, he'd doubted her love for the child and
pegged Devon as just another selfish woman like
Felicia. Why had it taken a tragedy to convince him
otherwise? All the love he had to give wouldn't be
enough to ease her heartache if Amanda was never
found. But he could try. As he observed Devon's suffering, he was prepared to risk his own life if only she
could be happy again.

He gave himself a mental shake to rid himself of his
Irish fatalism. The best he could do was help Devon
search for Amanda, because they couldn't live with
themselves if they didn't do everything possible to
recover the child.

After Betsy and his father returned to man the telephone with Wilcox, Colin wrapped a sweater around
Devon's shoulders and walked her to his truck.

At the drive-in, she declined a sandwich, but he
persuaded her to try a chocolate shake, which she

sipped as they drove through the nearly deserted streets.

"We'll start on the beach," he suggested, "and check the motel parking lots. Will you recognize the car if you see it?"

She nodded. "It's etched in my mind. I keep seeing it over and over, along with Amanda's empty playpen."

He cruised from one motel lot to another, easing slowly down each block so Devon could examine every parked car. They had about as much chance of finding the car as locating the proverbial needle in the haystack, but the process of searching had brought Devon out of her escalating depression. If he had to drive all night to keep her busy and her spirits up, he'd do it.

When their survey of the beach motels produced no results, he turned back toward the mainland.

"Where to now?" he asked.

She cradled her head in her hands as if her slender neck was too tired to support it. "I don't know. What kind of neighborhood does a kidnapper live in?"

He wanted to take her home and put her to bed where she belonged, but he knew she'd fight him. Better to keep her occupied until they heard something. "Maybe we should begin at the north end of town, near your house, then work south."

They scoured every block in her neighborhood, examined every parked car and every driveway before moving on to the next subdivision.

A little after midnight by the dashboard clock, she grabbed his arm. "Stop! I see it!"

He slammed on the brakes. "Where?"

"Back up. The driveway on the right."

He shifted into reverse and eased down the empty street. The dark hulk of an older-model Buick sat in the driveway of the house Devon indicated.

"That's it. That's the model." Her voice trembled with excitement and hope.

But when he turned into the driveway behind the car, his headlights illuminated the Buick's black paint.

"It looked green in the dark." Devon choked back a sob.

He backed onto the street, pulled the truck against the curb and reached over to massage the back of her neck. "You're all done in. Want to call it a night?"

She shook her head so fiercely she broke his hold on her. "I'll sleep when Amanda's found and not before."

"You're the boss." He switched on the radio to an easy-listening station, pressed the accelerator and resumed their search.

They had just picked up coffee at a McDonald's drive-through when the radio announcer began the hourly news broadcast. "The baby daughter of Amanda Donovan, nationally known child-care expert, was kidnapped two days ago from her home in the Tampa Bay area."

The newscaster continued with a description of Amanda and a number to call with information.

Devon's hands shook until her coffee sloshed onto her jeans. "The station must have taken the story off the wire services. Jake did as he promised."

"That's good. Now maybe the FBI will pick up some leads."

"Or the kidnapper will feel threatened and—"

"Stop it!" he lashed at her. "We're going to find Amanda and she's going to be fine."

"Do you really think so?" She turned toward him, and the sorrow in her eyes made him want to scream in frustration.

"Damn right. No doubt about it," he lied.

She attempted a brave smile that stabbed through him like a blade. "The sooner we get back to our search, the sooner we'll find her."

For another hour, they combed the streets while the city slept. They passed three green-and-white city police cars, a couple of winos huddled in an office doorway, a street sweeper with its lights flashing, several stray cats and an old man walking his dog. If the green Buick had been in town, it seemed to have vanished into thin air.

"Even if the car's still here, it could be parked in a garage," Colin said. "You need some rest. We can start again at first light."

She shook her head stubbornly. "We have to keep searching. We don't have a minute to waste—"

She went rigid with fright when his cell phone rang.

He flipped it open, never taking his eyes from her terrified gaze. When the call ended, he made a quick U-turn in the middle of the deserted street.

"We're going home." He reached across the wide seat and grasped her shoulder. "They've found her, and she's okay."

Chapter Thirteen

Being a mother demands unselfishness. Your child relies on you completely for his or her safety and well-being, and often you must give up what you want most to fulfill your obligation to your baby's security and happiness.
Amanda Donovan, *Bringing Up Baby*

Devon drew a blanket over Amanda, sleeping peacefully in her portable crib, sucking her thumb.

Guilt welled within her afresh, bubbling over and searing her with the reminder that Amanda wouldn't have been kidnapped if Devon hadn't been flirting with Colin in the attic. She'd proved herself to be the ultimate incompetent mother, one who'd allowed her child to be snatched from beneath her nose, not once, but three times.

"The FBI has no idea who took her?" she asked.

"We just finished debriefing the baby-sitter who brought her in," Stephen Wilcox said, amazingly fresh and alert for eight in the morning after a long night with little sleep. "We'd still be searching for Amanda if the local television station hadn't picked up her picture from the wire service and run it on the late-night news.''

"This is crazy." Colin, with his hands in the back pockets of his jeans, studied the child as she slept. "The sitter who saw Amanda's picture and called you has no idea who left her?"

"Not a clue," Wilcox said. "Claimed she usually checks out her clients thoroughly, but the woman who left the baby was in a hurry. She gave what appears to be a false name, said she was leaving immediately for Europe for three weeks—and offered to pay up front in cash."

"Wasn't the sitter suspicious?" Devon moved away from the crib, but perched on a chair close enough to keep the baby in sight.

Wilcox nodded. "She said the client's black-dyed hair, cheap clothes and coarse speech didn't fit the jet-set type, but the sitter's mother is in a nursing home, and the money was too good to turn down."

"Middle-aged, black hair, coarse speech." Colin gave Devon a questioning look. "Sound like anyone you know?"

Devon shook her head and tore her gaze from Amanda long enough to confront Wilcox. "Can you catch this woman?"

Wilcox stood and buttoned his jacket over his conservative tie. "Don't worry, Ms. Clarke, we're following every lead. We'll find her."

Her euphoria, created by Amanda's return, was dissipating rapidly in the morning light. Whoever had taken the baby was roaming free, perhaps even now waiting for a chance to snatch the child again. She forced a smile and a thank-you as Wilcox departed, while her thoughts wheeled with concern for Amanda's safety. She gasped in surprise as Colin encircled her waist from behind and nuzzled the back of her neck with kisses.

"No time for daydreams—or something even more pleasant." A mixture of suggestion and regret filled his voice. "Christmas will be here tomorrow."

"Good Lord." She broke from his embrace. "The interview! I forgot all about it. We'll never be ready in time."

"No problem. Dad and Betsy are unpacking decorations in the living room as we speak. And I'm off to find a tree."

They hadn't discussed what they would say to Sara Davis, the house wasn't decorated, she hadn't done the Christmas baking she'd planned for the show and she had no idea what she or Amanda would wear. She waited for panic to overtake her, but those responsibilities faded in importance when compared with Amanda's perilous situation. The interview—and her career—would have to take a back seat until Amanda's safety was assured.

"Everything will be fine." Colin pulled her against him, and the love shining in his eyes almost broke her resolve. He lowered his lips to hers, and for a brief moment, all care and pain receded as the warmth of his arms enfolded her.

But when he disappeared out the door, she rejected the traitorous longings of her heart and body and raced upstairs to her desk. After locating attorney John St. Clair's card, she called to Betsy to keep an eye on Amanda, then closed the door and picked up the telephone.

DEVON SMOOTHED the full-length, red-plaid taffeta skirt and adjusted the lace-edged cuffs of her silk blouse. Sara Davis's makeup artist had just applied a final touch of translucent powder to her face and tucked a holly sprig, tied with a red velvet ribbon, in her hair.

Sara, a tall, willowy blonde with bouffant, lacquered hair nodded her approval. "You have great visual appeal, Mrs. Donovan. And the house looks fantastic. I'll go over the final checklist with my director, and we'll begin shooting in about fifteen minutes."

Devon took a deep breath to calm the hyperactive butterflies dive-bombing in her stomach and prayed she hadn't forgotten something. Yesterday, with help from Mike and Betsy, she had banked every mantel and windowsill with pine boughs and waxy green magnolia leaves centered by tall bayberry candles. They had twined greenery and red velvet ribbon along the banister in the hall and around the front entrance. With assistance from Betty Crocker and the Pillsbury Doughboy, she'd hastily baked and decorated Christmas cakes and cookies, filling the house with delectable aromas of cinnamon and sugar that blended with the sharp scent of pine boughs.

Colin had secured the Florida pine in the corner by the fireplace and draped it with multiple strings of tiny white lights. Together they'd added handmade Victorian decorations of lace and velvet. She'd worked until the wee hours of the morning to prepare the house for Sara Davis's cameras, and when she finally fell across her bed to sleep, she'd been so exhausted she hadn't known whether Colin slept beside her or not.

He hadn't been there when she awakened a few hours ago, and she hadn't seen him all morning, although she'd heard him calling through the house to his dad and Betsy, who scurried to help with last-minute details.

Surrounded by the sights and smells of Christmas and with carols played by hand bells drifting through the rooms from the sound system, Devon swallowed hard to clear the knot in her throat. She was moving through a perfect fantasy of family, companionship, happiness and love, the life she'd dreamed of when she'd celebrated solitary Christmases with Aunt Bessie. And like all dreams, this one wouldn't last. As soon as the Davis interview was finished and Colin discovered her plans for Amanda, she would find herself alone again.

Betsy popped her head into the bedroom, breaking into Devon's daydreams. "Someone named John St. Clair to see you. I told him you were busy, but he insists it's urgent. I put him in the dining room."

With a rustle of her taffeta skirt, Devon followed Betsy downstairs.

"Where's Colin?" Devon asked.

Betsy shrugged. "Last time I saw him, he was out in the garage, arranging tools on the workbench."

"Tell him Sara wants to begin in fifteen minutes," Devon said. "I'll get rid of St. Clair."

She stepped over cables the size of her wrist that snaked through the hall and into the living room, where Sara's crew had set up their cameras, lights and huge umbrella-shaped reflectors. In the dining room, St. Clair paced before the windows.

"What is it?" she asked.

The young attorney straightened the knot of his silk tie and squared his shoulders. "I apologize for interrupting. I tried to call—"

"We've disconnected the phones so they won't ring during filming." Her heart fluttered with a curious mixture of anticipation and dread. "Have you found a family?"

He nodded. "The Watsons. Exactly what you wanted. Mother and father and two siblings. They want to meet with you and the baby as soon as possible. Is day after tomorrow at ten o'clock all right?"

Events were moving too fast. Although she'd accepted the fact that she couldn't keep Amanda, the thought of losing her within days stabbed her with a pain so intense she grabbed the back of a dining chair for support.

"They want to take the child immediately," St. Clair explained, "before she forms an attachment."

Too late. She pictured the expression on Amanda's face whenever she entered the baby's field of vision. When the child was kidnapped, Devon had experienced what life without Amanda would be like and knew she'd formed a deep and lasting attachment of her own.

I have to get hold of myself. If I didn't love the child so much, I wouldn't be giving her up. It's her safety, not my feelings that matter here.

"Day after tomorrow will be fine." She forced the painful words through wooden lips.

"I'll notify the Watsons," he said.

When she turned to accompany him to the door, she encountered Colin on the dining-room threshold, leaning against the doorjamb with his arms folded across his chest. The smoldering fury in his eyes warned her that he'd overheard her instructions to the lawyer.

"I'll show myself out." St. Clair took in Colin's expression and hastened from the room.

Her heart sank as she faced Colin. "I can explain—"

"Don't bother." The outrage revealed by his cold, measured tone matched the anger in his eyes. "What you're doing is perfectly clear."

She'd expected this reaction, had prepared herself for losing both him and the child, but she hadn't anticipated the depth of agony those losses would bring. He would leave her anyway, but he had to understand she wasn't like Felicia.

"I did it for—" she began.

Sara Davis stepped into the dining room. "Show time, Mr. and Mrs. Donovan. Let's get started."

At Sara's appearance, all emotion disappeared from Colin's face, and with a coolness that froze Devon's heart, he motioned her to precede him through the maze of cables and light stands into the living room.

Betsy appeared with Amanda, who immediately stretched out her arms toward Devon and smacked her lips in an attempt to speak. "Ma-ma-ma-ma."

Devon's heart reeled at the sound, and she reached for the child, whose arms clasped her neck in a ferocious hug.

"It's easy to see she's crazy about her mother," Sara observed.

"The two are inseparable, isn't that right, dear?" Colin, dressed in new jeans, a plaid shirt and a red pullover sweater, settled on the sofa and extended his long legs. The gray in his eyes glinted like ice water.

As Devon occupied the sofa beside him with Amanda wiggling on her lap, she flinched at the trace of bitterness in his voice.

"Both of you relax," Sara said with a smile obviously intended to put them at ease, "and we'll just have a nice chat while the camera's rolling. Don't worry if things seem out of sequence or if you have to repeat something. Everything will be carefully edited."

The world-famous talk-show host, elegant in a Dior suit the color of spun gold, sat in the wing chair opposite them and crossed her long, slender legs to exhibit sheer stockings dusted with golden glitter that matched her designer outfit.

"The first thing our viewers will want to know," she stated in her silky trademark voice, "is that your baby is safe and sound. The country was devastated by the news of her kidnapping."

Amanda turned in Devon's lap and patted her cheek, and tears welled in Devon's eyes at the memory of Amanda's disappearance. Colin shifted toward her and placed an arm around her shoulder, drawing her close.

"We're grateful to the media and the FBI," he said, "for their help in returning our daughter to us. The days she was gone were the worst of our lives."

"I can understand," Sara said. "She's a real sweetheart."

On the monitor, Devon watched the camera zoom in on Amanda, dressed in dark green velvet with a white bertha collar, white tights and black patent Mary Jane shoes. She'd tugged her green velvet headband with its matching bow over one eye and sat sucking contentedly on three fingers of her left hand. Instinctively, Devon tightened her grip on the child and thrust away thoughts of the upcoming adoption.

"Your baby is only seven months old," Sara observed, "but you've been writing your column for years. How did you learn so much about babies?"

Under the hot glare of the lights, Devon's mind went blank and a trickle of perspiration slithered down her spine.

"My wife is a voracious reader," Colin said, jumping in to fill the silence. "She wanted to learn all she could about child care before having children of our own."

Devon held her breath, fearing he would reveal the secret of Gramma's journals.

"And," he continued, "she's an astute observer of human behavior."

Devon let out the breath she hadn't realized she was holding, then tensed again at his next words.

"Since the baby came—" he fixed Devon with an ambiguous grin "—you could say she's followed the trial-and-error method, learning firsthand what works and what doesn't."

Sara leaned forward, interest flashing in her sapphire eyes. "And how did your theories stand up under practical application?"

Anxiety set in again as Devon recalled the frustrations of changing diapers, disastrous feedings and futile attempts to quiet a fretting Amanda. But she couldn't admit those failures on network television. The syndicate, which paid her to convince readers how simple motherhood could be, would fire her.

Amanda wiggled on her lap, and the waterproof covering of her disposable diaper crinkled. Devon hugged the child for coming to her rescue. "There is one bit of advice I've reconsidered, and that's the use of disposable diapers. Whenever possible, mothers should use washable ones, but I can't deny the times when the convenience of disposables outweighs all other factors."

"Spoken like a true pragmatist." Colin patted her shoulder and beamed at her with another ambiguous smile.

If he was implying her decision to place Amanda in a safe home was strictly practical, he'd better think again. She reminded herself that his anger grew out of his disappointment and suppressed the desire to wipe the smug grin off his face. Such antisocial behavior might be desirable on "Geraldo," but neither Sara nor the syndicate would approve.

"Let's back up a bit," Sara said. "Tell me how you two met."

"How we met?" Devon focused on an elegant papier-mâché angel, dressed in golden gauze and lace, that stood in the center of the mantelpiece. "We, uh, met—"

"In the hardware store," Colin chimed in. "In the paint section. She was dressed in these cute little denim shorts and an oversize T-shirt. She looked like a teenager."

Sara nodded with approval. "And was it love at first sight?"

"No," Devon insisted immediately.

"Of course," Colin said at the same time.

Amanda wriggled impatiently, and Devon set her on the rug beside the sofa.

"Well, which was it?" Sara asked with an amused grin.

Devon felt her eyes widen with alarm as she looked to Colin to rescue her and prayed that in his anger and disappointment he wouldn't blow her cover. For a brief, shining moment, his face reflected warmth and compassion before his bland expression settled in once again.

"It was just as we said," he explained. "I fell in love with my wife the instant I saw her, but it took a little time to convince her she felt the same about me."

Sara turned to Devon. "And how did he do that?"

Devon kept her gaze on Colin. "By showing me how much he loves children and family. And by how well he cooks."

Sara laughed. "What woman wouldn't love a man who can cook? And how long have you been married now?"

"Let's see." Colin began counting on his fingers. "It's been five—"

"Years," Devon broke in. "Five years last—"

"Week," Colin interrupted. "We celebrated our anniversary just last week."

Sara nodded. "And how does America's most celebrated couple observe an anniversary?"

"With dinner and dancing—" Devon began.

"At the beach where we were married," Colin finished.

Sara tapped her lips with a gold-lacquered nail. "Do you always finish each other's sentences?"

"Not always—" Devon started to reply.

"But when you've been married as long as we have," Colin said, casting Devon a look laden with double meaning, "you always know what the other is thinking."

Devon tore her gaze away from his accusing eyes and looked to Amanda at her feet, but the child wasn't there. A quick survey of the room revealed Amanda racing on hands and knees toward the Christmas tree in the corner.

Devon leaped from the sofa toward the child, too late to prevent Amanda from grabbing hold of the tree's lower limb to pull herself up. Devon snatched the child into her arms and out of harm's way just before the tree tottered precariously as if in slow motion, then fell with a resounding crash of branches and the tinkle of breaking ornaments.

The last image Devon observed as the tree neared the floor was the cameraman, jumping nimbly to swing the camera to capture Sara Davis's horrified expression just before the tree engulfed her in its decorated branches.

Colin sprang to his feet and lifted the tree off the world-famous television personality.

"Are you all right?" Devon asked her.

Sara parted the strands of tinsel that hid her eyes. "I believe this segment of our interview is finished."

Chapter Fourteen

The greatest gift a mother and father can give
their child is to love each other.
Amanda Donovan, *Bringing Up Baby*

Colin welcomed the cold blast of air-conditioned air
as he entered his father's kitchen and loosened his tie.
He'd spent a long, frustrating day searching for office headquarters for his architectural firm, and all
he'd achieved was sore ears from an overtalkative
real-estate agent.

At least at home his ears would get a rest. His father had barely spoken to him since he had walked out
on Devon Clarke the minute Sara Davis's crew pulled
away two weeks ago.

He discovered his dad leaning against the kitchen
counter, staring at his mother's cheerful smile among
the photographs on the bulletin board.

Mike shifted his gaze to greet him with a look that
boded bad news. "May God and your sainted mother
forgive me, but I can see I've raised an imbecile."

Colin slumped in a chair, propped his elbows on the table and raked his fingers through his hair. "Aren't things bad enough without your sarcasm?"

"And whose fault is that?"

Colin felt the anger reddening his face. "You don't think it's *my* fault?"

His father opened a cabinet, removed a bottle of Irish whiskey and two glasses and sat opposite him. "That's exactly what I'm thinking. You're the one who rushed out of the house after the interview, speaking to the poor girl only long enough to instruct her to mail your check."

"But—"

"You're the one who hasn't spoken to her in over two weeks." Mike splashed whiskey into both glasses and slid one across the table.

Colin ignored the drink, folded his arms on the table and leaned toward his father. "I'm not the one who put Amanda up for adoption or used the poor kid just long enough for an interview to boost my bloody career or pretended I cared about the baby, then passed her off to the first couple who wanted her."

Mike downed his whiskey in a gulp and slammed his glass on the table. "If you believe that, son, you're even dumber than I thought."

Colin waited for the surge of virtuous indignation, the permeating sense of the rightness of what he'd done. He'd felt bitterness but no regrets when he'd cut his ties with Felicia, but walking away from Devon hadn't brought the same satisfaction. Instead, he suffered a chronic feeling of unease, like a bed of nettles had taken root in his heart.

To fuel his anger, he shoved away memories of Devon in his arms, her puckish smile and her tender care of Amanda, and clung instead to the picture of her, conspiring with the attorney to send Amanda away. She'd fooled him once. He wouldn't allow her to bamboozle him again. He hardened his heart and glared at his father. "What else am I supposed to think?"

"How about the truth?" Mike grinned, his good humor evidently restored by the belt of liquor. "There're holes in your conclusions big enough to drive a Caterpillar earth mover through."

"What kind of holes?" He realized his father's good-natured smile wasn't whiskey induced, but the same expression the old man sported when he held a winning poker hand.

"I take it you know all about the child's trust fund?" Mike asked with the feigned innocence of a cardsharp.

"What trust fund?"

His father shrugged. "More than enough money to support Devon Clarke and Amanda for the rest of their days. And it's all under Devon's control."

Uneasiness pricked Colin. "What difference does the money make?"

His father circled the rim of his glass with his finger. "Seems to me if Devon is the career-conscious, money-grubbing gold digger you claim, keeping the child *and* the money would have paid off in the long run. There was enough to pay a full-time nanny and still have tons of cash to spare.''

"Are you saying Devon was making money off the baby?'' Colin's anger boiled through him with fresh strength.

Mike shook his head. "Devon refuses to touch a cent of the trust fund. Put it all in an account for the child. And she is well aware whoever adopts the child will also keep the money, although she plans to keep that fact hidden until she's located the right family.''

"If she has all that money, why is she so anxious to get rid of Amanda?''

Mike tapped his forehead with his index finger. "Now you're grinding the old brain into gear. *You* figure it out.''

Images of Devon's tear-streaked face when Amanda disappeared and her joy at the child's return flashed through Colin's mind, and the answer hit him like a ton of bricks.

How could he have been so dense not to see it? He'd let his experience with Felicia color his assessment of Devon, causing him to jump to all the wrong conclusions. His own stupid pride had kept him from understanding Devon's motivations, from acknowledging she loved Amanda so much that she'd give the child up to keep her safe.

He lifted his gaze to meet his father's. "She was afraid for Amanda.''

"Blessed Jesus, Mary and Joseph,'' his father sighed with a dramatic roll of his eyes. "I didn't sire an imbecile after all. Of course she was afraid. Three times somebody tried to take the child. Devon wants

Amanda far away with a new identity where no one can harm her. Too bad now her good intentions are all too late."

Colin's head snapped up, and he fixed his father with a piercing stare. "What do you mean, 'too late'?"

Mike's grin faded into a scowl. "Before Amanda's adoption by the Watsons could be finalized, Ernest Potts, the half uncle, sued for custody, claiming Devon's an unfit mother."

"Devon's a wonderful mother," Colin insisted. "The man must be crazy."

Mike raised his bushy white brows. "Or greedy. He knows if he gets Amanda, he gets the trust fund, too."

Colin groaned and buried his face in his hands. "I've made a terrible mistake."

"That you have, son." Mike nodded solemnly. "Now what are you going to do about it?"

DEVON SHIFTED in the hard wooden chair and fought against claustrophobia. The courtroom was nothing like the airy chambers with tall windows on old "Perry Mason" reruns. Its dropped ceiling with flickering fluorescent lights, cramped, windowless space and musty carpet seemed like a foretaste of prison.

She smoothed the skirt of the pastel floral dress St. Clair had suggested she wear. Something demure and maternal, he'd said, to impress the judge. She grimaced at the irony of her situation. She'd come to court to fight like hell to keep Amanda long enough to give her away again.

At the sound of people approaching across the aisle, she glanced up and met the gaze of a balding, middle-aged man with piglike eyes. Ernest Potts! He pulled out a chair for a woman with bleached-blond hair.

Devon's memories clicked like a high-speed computer. She'd seen them both before—Ernest on her street in his green Buick the day Amanda had arrived, and his wife in the department store the day Amanda disappeared. In that instant, she knew without doubt the two of them had been responsible for every attempt to take Amanda from her.

She leaned toward St. Clair and whispered her deductions in his ear. "If we can prove they're responsible, we'll win our case."

And I can keep Amanda! With the Pottses behind bars, she'll be safe. And in her heart she knew, even in her worst maternal moments, she'd be a better parent than either of the Pottses.

She tried not to think of Colin, who'd walked away two months ago without giving her a chance to explain her rationale for Amanda's adoption. The ache in her heart stole her breath, and she attempted to console herself with the prospect of single motherhood.

"It may be too late," St. Clair whispered in her ear and helped lift her to her feet by her elbow. "The judge is coming in now, and we have no evidence to support your allegations."

After the judge had seated himself at the bench, Devon settled back into her chair and leaned toward St. Clair. "I can testify that I saw them in our neighborhood and at the department store where Amanda was taken," she murmured.

"All circumstantial," he mumbled in a low voice and rose to his feet again. "Yes, we're ready, Your Honor."

For the next three hours, she listened and squirmed as Potts's attorney called police and security personnel forward. All testified that Amanda had disappeared while under Devon's care. The fire chief testified that it was her apparent carelessness that had caused the fire at her house the day of Amanda's arrival.

Then the seedy lawyer called Mrs. Kaplan to the stand. The dear old lady came forward, threw Devon an apologetic glance and took her seat beside the judge. She fidgeted like a water drop on a griddle and twisted the lavender skirt of her best dress with nervous fingers.

"Mrs. Kaplan," Potts's lawyer crooned in an oily voice, "you reside across the street from Ms. Clarke?"

Mrs. Kaplan nodded nervously.

The judge dropped his gruff expression and smiled at the older woman. "Please answer aloud for the record."

"Yes, I do." She looked over at Devon and lifted her shoulders in a helpless shrug.

Devon nodded encouragement, but her heart sank as the older woman described how Devon's car with Amanda in it had ended up on her front lawn. Mrs. Kaplan left the stand, unable this time to meet Devon's glance.

Potts leaned forward in his seat beside his attorney and smirked at Devon with a malicious grin. His wife, appearing uncomfortable, refused to look her way.

Devon huddled with St. Clair. "You have to do *something*. They've made me look worse than Cinderella's stepmother."

St. Clair's demeanor was calm, but she could read the frustration in his tone. "If you have some solid evidence to disprove any of this, let's have it now."

"I can't disprove it—it all happened," she muttered through gritted teeth, "but I *know* Potts was behind it. Can't you ask for a delay?"

He nodded. "I'll see what I can do."

She cast another sideways glance at the couple seated at the table across the aisle and quashed a shudder. She couldn't allow those two to take Amanda. Their coarseness and bad manners offended her, but more than that, the couple lacked honesty and decency. What kind of environment would they provide for her little angel?

In the air-conditioned stuffiness of the room, she could almost feel Amanda's tiny body snuggled against her, the plump arms encircling her neck, the pudgy palm patting her cheek while the precious voice whispered "Mama" in her ear. Too late, she realized she could never give the baby up, not even to the most qualified adoptive parents in the world. In a few brief months, Amanda had become *her* child, and she would fight until her last breath to keep her.

The opposing lawyer stood and approached the bench, and Ernest Potts caught her eye and flashed a triumphant grin.

Good Lord, what are they up to now?

The lawyer hooked his thumbs in the vest of his outdated three-piece suit and strutted like a bantam cock before the bench. "Your Honor, we intend to prove not only that Ms. Clarke is negligent in her responsibilities toward her ward, but also that she is a woman of loose character and poor moral fiber."

Devon flinched as if she'd been struck.

The smug little man turned and pointed his finger at her. "This woman cohabited for weeks with a man who is not her husband, but worse than that, this incompetent guardian has foisted herself upon the American public as baby-care expert, Amanda Donovan."

A collective gasp arose in the courtroom, and for the first time, Devon was aware of the small group of spectators who filled the tiny room behind her. Footsteps scurried up the aisle and the courtroom door slammed. A reporter, no doubt, off to call in the scoop.

Her stomach churned and her hands turned to ice. Her career no longer mattered. The syndicate could fire her if they wished. All she could think of was Amanda, safe and secure at home now with Betsy and Mike, but not for long. What Potts's attorney had claimed about Colin staying at her house and her fooling the public with her column was all too true.

St. Clair jumped to his feet. "We ask for a continuance, Your Honor, to dispute these allegations."

"Request denied." The grim-faced judge scorched her with a disapproving look and consulted his watch.

"But it is close to the lunch hour. We'll recess until two o'clock."

He dismissed the court with a bang of his gavel that shattered Devon's heart. She'd lost everything now. After disentangling Sara Davis from the fallen Christmas tree, Colin had walked out of her life forever, and soon her darling Amanda would leave, not for a safe and happy home, but to provide a greedy aunt and uncle with her trust fund.

Devon laid her head on her folded arms, blocking out the sickly, flickering lights and ignoring the buzz of voices beside her.

Through the haze of pain, a hand gripped her shoulder. "Devon?"

Colin's voice. Her agony at losing Amanda had driven her over the edge, and she was suffering auditory hallucinations.

Strong hands lifted her by the elbows and turned her around. She looked up into Colin's face.

"I love you, Devon, and everything's going to be all right." He crushed her in his powerful embrace and his lips grazed her forehead before he released her and stepped away. "Now I want you to meet two very important people."

She glanced to the end of the table where St. Clair was conferring with two strangers.

The first, a stocky young man in faded jeans and a leather motorcycle jacket, turned toward her. A diamond stud flashed in his right ear as he extended a meaty paw toward her. "Sam Janowsky. Pleased to meetcha."

"Sam's a private investigator," Colin explained. "He's been researching this case with me for the past six weeks."

Colin motioned to the distinguished, gray-haired gentleman in an Armani suit, who broke off his intense conversation with St. Clair to offer his hand. The strength of his grip belied his mild appearance. "Don't worry, Ms. Clarke. We won't let them take your child."

Colin eased her into a chair just as her knees threatened to buckle. "William Wollencroft just flew in from Philadelphia. He's the country's best legal expert in child custody cases." Colin nodded to the newcomers. "You have your work cut out for you during the recess, gentlemen."

St. Clair, appearing as stunned as she felt, motioned them up the aisle. "My office is in the next building. I'll have lunch delivered while we confer."

Devon shook her head, too punchy from the rapid chain of events to think straight. Like a drowning swimmer who'd gone under for the third time, only to be snatched from the watery jaws of death at the last minute, she clung to Colin's arm. "Who hired those two?"

He pulled her against the comforting breadth of his chest, and her shivers eased. "I did, several weeks ago."

She tipped her head to search for traces of the outrage he'd exhibited at their last meeting, but found only affection shining in his eyes. "Why didn't you tell me? I thought I'd never see you again."

His arms tightened around her shoulders. "Gathering all the information we needed took most of my time—and I didn't want you to know how dirty these proceedings might be."

She nodded, content, and pressed her cheek against his thudding heart. A question formed in her mind, and she raised her head to confront him once more. "Philadelphia lawyers and private investigators are expensive. Who's paying for all this?"

"Don't you remember?" He kissed the tip of her nose. "I made a bundle off the Sara Davis interview."

Tears filled her eyes. For the past weeks, all the time she'd thought she'd lost him forever, he'd been thinking of her and Amanda and working to keep them together. If hearts ever exploded with love, hers was a prime candidate.

He released her and pointed toward the door. "As much as I've wanted to hold you for weeks, there's something more important we have to take care of before court reconvenes."

"What is it?" she asked over her shoulder as she preceded him up the aisle.

"A surprise." He pushed her gently to quicken her pace. "But you'll have to skip lunch."

WHEN COURT RECONVENED, Colin took his place beside Devon at the table before the judge, and Wollencroft joined St. Clair.

When Potts's lawyer had finished presenting his case, Wollencroft moved into action like a well-oiled, precision machine. "I call Sam Janowsky to the stand."

Sam swore to tell the truth and took the witness chair, filling the box with his muscled bulk.

"Mr. Janowsky," Wollencroft began, "I understand that, in your capacity as a private investigator, you have traced the whereabouts of Ernest and Muriel Potts, who swore earlier under oath that they had not left the state of Missouri for the past six months."

Janowsky nodded, pulled a tattered notebook from his jacket pocket and responded, "After securing photographs of the Pottses and the license number of their car, I interviewed every motel owner in the county. The manager of the Crooked Palm Motel informed me the Pottses were registered there for a four-week period from late September through most of October."

Potts's lawyer sprang to his feet. "Objection. Hearsay, Your Honor."

The judge looked to Wollencroft with raised eyebrows.

"We have a sworn affidavit from the manager and a copy of his register, Your Honor. And the manager is willing to come forward to testify in person, if needed."

"Objection overruled," the judge intoned.

For the next hour, the courtroom rang with objections from the plaintiff's lawyer as Janowsky and Wollencroft presented a sheaf of affidavits, placing Potts, his wife and their green Buick in Devon's neighborhood time after time. The crushing blow came when the baby-sitter, who had cared for

Amanda after her kidnapping, took the stand and identified Muriel Potts as the woman who'd brought her the child, claiming the baby as her own.

Potts slumped in his chair, fixing Devon with a twisted scowl, but his sour looks couldn't harm her now. With her hand clasped tightly in Colin's, she watched Potts's lawyer's last-ditch attempt to discredit her.

"Even if my clients did take the child," he explained in a wheedling tone, "they did it for the baby's own good. Ms. Clarke was a poor mother and living with a man she wasn't married to."

A victorious smile flitted briefly across Wollencroft's face when he called Colin as a witness. "Please tell the court, Mr. O'Reilly, your firsthand observations of Ms. Clarke's parenting skills."

As Colin answered, his gaze locked with hers, and her eyes welled with happy tears at his words. "Devon is an exceptional mother. The years of writing her column, 'Bringing Up Baby,' have provided her with a wealth of information to supplement her inherent love and devotion to Amanda. In fact, she is so well qualified, I have asked her to be the mother of my children."

Potts and his lawyer exchanged a pleased look, as if Colin had fallen into their trap, but their expressions changed at Wollencroft's next question.

"And just what *is* your relationship to Devon Clarke?"

Colin dug into the inside pocket of his jacket and produced a piece of paper. "Devon Clarke is my wife."

He handed the judge the marriage license, signed just two hours before in Judge Batsford's chambers, where they had been married, with Mike, Betsy, Mrs. Kaplan and Amanda as witnesses.

"And as soon as Devon's guardianship of Amanda is settled," Colin continued, "we want to begin official adoption proceedings for Amanda."

A rumble of applause broke out among the spectators, and the judge banged his gavel for order. But Devon heard and saw nothing but Colin, whose expression promised her all she'd ever longed for in life.

"YOU'LL HAVE TO PUT ME down to open the door," Devon said with a giggle.

Colin tightened his grip beneath her knees. "A bride should be carried across the threshold—"

"I know, for luck. But since you're holding me in both your arms, how can you unlock the suite?"

His face assumed stern lines as she shifted her weight in his embrace. "One of the first lessons you should learn, Mrs. O'Reilly, is that marriage is a cooperative venture."

"Of course." She mimicked his solemn expression and reached into his breast pocket for the room card. "I never can figure out which way these things should be inserted."

He nibbled at her ear. "Just be quick about it, okay?"

She drew back and gazed at the heated look in his smoky eyes. "Am I too heavy for you?"

"I assure you, dear wife, that my haste arises from another source."

"Arises, does it?" She laughed again as the door swung open.

He swept her down the narrow entrance hall and into the living room of the suite. Curtains billowed around sliding glass doors that opened to the gulf, framing the setting sun. She stepped onto the balcony, where the sea breeze lifted her hair and cooled her skin. Colin stood behind her, drawing her against him.

"Shall we order dinner?" she kidded, vibrantly aware of her growing need and his hard arousal pressed against her.

"Whatever you wish," he murmured in her ear. "I want to spend the rest of my life pleasing you."

She turned in the circle of his arms and lifted her face to his. "What you did for me—for us—today pleases me enough for a lifetime."

"I love you, Devon." His kiss drove away all other thoughts and she was aware only of the heat of his flesh against hers, the taste of him, the desire that consumed her like a white flame. "Let's have dinner later." The passion in his face reflected her own.

"Why postpone dinner?" she teased again. "We've already had our wedding night."

He scooped her into his arms again and carried her through the living room toward the bedroom. "That was just a trial run. Tonight, my love, is the real thing."

Epilogue

One year later

Leona gazed out her office window at snowflakes billowing down the canyon formed by the tall buildings of Forty-second Street. The city was in for a white Christmas.

"Here's your coffee." Gwen, her secretary for the past fifteen years, placed a Meissen cup and saucer filled with the steaming brew in the center of the desk blotter and bustled across the room to fold back the bookcase doors, revealing a television set.

Leona swiveled her chair from the window, glanced at the small gold clock on her desk and threw Gwen a grateful smile. "Right on time, as always."

Gwen handed her the remote control. "I'll hold all your calls for the next hour."

As soon as the door closed behind her secretary, Leona unzipped her knee-high boots of red Italian leather, kicked them off, propped her stockinged feet on a pulled-out bottom drawer and switched on the TV.

The sound of feel-good orchestral music with a catchy beat filled the room as the picture brightened. Leona reached for her coffee cup with a smile of satisfaction. That sound was money in the bank.

The program's opening scene panned the front of Devon's old Victorian home, gleaming now with authentic turn-of-the-century colors on its shingles and trim, then the camera moved up the walk, taking in the landscape plantings and perfectly trimmed lawn. As if by magic, the double doors of leaded, beveled glass swung open, and the film began documenting the attractive, comfortable-looking living room and the dining room set with the best china and silver, as if for company.

In the kitchen, the shot tightened on yellow geraniums on the windowsill, racks of copper cookware and an artistic display of fruit, spices and utensils on the counter. Finally, the camera swung to the family room, where Colin and Devon stood before the fireplace with an almost-two-year-old Amanda in her father's arms.

"Welcome back to the O'Reillys'," Devon greeted the viewers, "where Colin, Amanda and I are always happy to have you visit."

The theme music swelled again before the program cut for its first commercial. Leona muted the sound and sipped her coffee, silently adding up her commission on the newly syndicated show. It had been a close call with Devon. They'd almost lost the column when the story of Devon's true identity broke.

"We owe everything to Jake Blalock," Devon had insisted when the media frenzy died down. "If he hadn't assigned his best reporter to write a sympathetic story of Amanda's adoption and our marriage for the wire services, things might have turned out differently.''

Good old Jake. The response to that story had sent the Nielsen ratings for the Sara Davis interview over the top, and Colin and Devon's own weekly show, "No Place Like Home," had gone into production almost immediately. Not to mention the twenty percent rise in the number of newspapers that carried *Bringing Up Baby*.

Leona turned up the volume as the program returned, and Colin's handsome face filled the screen.

"Today," he said, "I'm putting the finishing touches on the in-law apartment I began in September."

Leona watched Colin fasten crown moldings and hang doors. All over the country, women without a smidgen of interest in carpentry were glued to their sets for a glimpse of the man who had ridden into the courtroom like a knight on a white horse, rescuing Amanda from the clutches of the unscrupulous Ernest Potts and sweeping Devon off her feet into marriage and a respectability that redeemed her career.

After Colin made the final adjustments to the door hardware, the camera panned the bare room. "Next week, you'll see what my wife's decorating skills can do with this empty space." His voice softened on *wife,* just enough to make every female viewer swoon with envy. "And then the room will be ready for occupancy."

Occupancy. Leona chuckled. As a frequent visitor to the O'Reilly household, she'd be the only occupant. Colin and Devon had planned the addition as a surprise, an in-law apartment for Mike. Mike had countered with a surprise of his own. He'd married Mrs. Kaplan, and now the two were honeymooning in Bermuda.

During the next commercial, Gwen slipped in and took a seat. She always watched part of the program on her morning coffee break.

"Devon's putting on a little weight, don't you think?" Gwen asked, as they observed the cooking segment in which Devon, assisted by Amanda in a red-checked pinafore, baked and decorated Christmas cookies.

Leona nodded. "Contentment does that to a woman."

When the program ended and the shot tightened on the family threesome again, the O'Reillys previewed next week's program.

"Join us," Colin said, with his arm around Devon's shoulder and his other hand caressing Amanda's curls, "when I demonstrate how to construct a cradle—"

"And I model the latest in maternity fashions," Devon added. The camera pulled in for a final close-up of the couple. Their faces glowed with joy. "You see, we'll be bringing up another baby come June."

"And always remember," Colin said, "that there's 'No Place Like Home.'" He pulled Devon into his arms and kissed her as the credits rolled.

With a satisfied sigh, Leona leaned back in her chair and savored the happiness of the family on the screen. She'd always been a sucker for happy endings.

BRIDE'S BAY RESORT

UNLOCK THE DOOR TO GREAT ROMANCE AT BRIDE'S BAY RESORT

Join Harlequin's new across-the-lines series, set in an exclusive hotel on an island off the coast of South Carolina.

Seven of your favorite authors will bring you exciting stories about fascinating heroes and heroines discovering love at Bride's Bay Resort.

Look for these fabulous stories coming to a store near you beginning in January 1996.

Harlequin American Romance #613 in January
Matchmaking Baby by Cathy Gillen Thacker

Harlequin Presents #1794 in February
Indiscretions by Robyn Donald

Harlequin Intrigue #362 in March
Love and Lies by Dawn Stewardson

Harlequin Romance #3404 in April
Make Believe Engagement by Day Leclaire

Harlequin Temptation #588 in May
Stranger in the Night by Roseanne Williams

Harlequin Superromance #695 in June
Married to a Stranger by Connie Bennett

Harlequin Historicals #324 in July
Dulcie's Gift by Ruth Langan

Visit Bride's Bay Resort each month wherever
Harlequin books are sold.

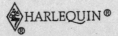

HARLEQUIN®

BBAYG

MILLION DOLLAR SWEEPSTAKES

SWP-H296

*With only forty-eight hours to lasso their mates—
it's a stampede...to the altar!*

by Cathy Gillen Thacker

Looking down from above, Montana maven
Max McKendrick wants to make sure his heirs get
something money can't buy—true love! And if his two
nephews and niece want to inherit their piece of his
sprawling Silver Spur ranch then they'll have to wed the
spouse of *his* choice—within forty-eight hours!

Don't miss any of the Wild West Weddings titles!

#625 THE COWBOY'S BRIDE (April)

#629 THE RANCH STUD (May)

#633 THE MAVERICK MARRIAGE (June)

Fall in love all over again with

This Time... MARRIAGE

In this collection of original short stories, three brides get a unique chance for a return engagement!

- Being kidnapped from your bridal shower by a one-time love can really put a crimp in your wedding plans! *The Borrowed Bride*— by **Susan Wiggs,** *Romantic Times* Career Achievement Award-winning author.

- After fifteen years a couple reunites for the sake of their child—this time will it end in marriage? *The Forgotten Bride*—by **Janice Kaiser.**

- It's tough to make a good divorce stick—especially when you're thrown together with your ex in a magazine wedding shoot! *The Bygone Bride*— by **Muriel Jensen.**

Don't miss THIS TIME...MARRIAGE, available in April wherever Harlequin books are sold.

HARLEQUIN ®

STEP

INTO

THE

A collection of award-winning books
by award-winning authors!
From Harlequin and Silhouette.

Available this April

TOGETHER ALWAYS

by DALLAS SCHULZE

Voted Best American Romance—
Reviewer's Choice Award

Award-winning author Dallas Schulze brings you the romantic
tale of two people destined to be together. From the moment
he laid eyes on her, Trace Dushane knew he had but one
mission in life...to protect beautiful Lily. He promised to save
her from disaster, but could he save her from himself?

Dallas Schulze is "one of today's most exciting authors!"
—Barbara Bretton

Available this April wherever Harlequin books are sold.

The Magic Wedding Dress

Imagine a wedding dress that costs a million dollars. Imagine a wedding dress that allows the wearer to find her one true love—not always the man she thinks it is. And then imagine a wedding dress that brings out all the best attributes in its bride, so that every man who glimpses her is sure to fall in love. Karen Toller Whittenburg imagined just such a dress and allowed it to take on a life of its own in her new American Romance trilogy, *The Magic Wedding Dress*. Be sure to catch all three:

March
#621—THE MILLION-DOLLAR BRIDE

May
#630—THE FIFTY-CENT GROOM

August
#643—THE TWO-PENNY WEDDING

Come along and dream with Karen Toller Whittenburg!

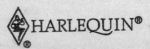